To Joe

A COWBOY'S ODYESSY

By Thomas G. Walmsley

Thomas G. Walmsley
(GARY)

© 2006

ISBN- 13: 978-1478257295

ISBN- 10: 1478257296

All rights reserved. No part of this publication may be reproduced or transmitted in any form or by any means, electronic or mechanical, including photocopy, recording, or any information storage and retrieval system, without prior written permission in writing from the author.

All characters are a figment of my imagination.

~ T.G. Walmsley

Requests for permission to make copies of any part of the work should be submitted to the following address:

Permissions Department, 5530 Melanie Lane Oscoda, MI 48750

Dedicated to my beautiful wife, Mary Jane

and our extended family,

T.G.W.

CHAPTER ONE

Walt Sanger entered the horse barn. His young son Orin was working hard at mucking out the stalls. Walt was so proud of his boy that he felt he would burst with emotion.

He said, "Orin you've been out here all morning, take a break and clean up. We'll eat lunch and then take a ride and check the fences."

"Okay, Pa," Orin replied.

While Orin was cleaning up, Walt thought about his wife Myra. She went to Abilene with Cal, their foreman, and four of the ranch hands. They took about one hundred head of cattle and the chuck wagon. Myra was going to do some shopping and stock up on supplies while the men took care of business. Walt smiled when he thought of Myra riding in the chuck wagon - she sure was feisty.

Walt and Orin ate a quick meal and saddled up their mounts for the inspection of the fences. It was a beautiful day and they enjoyed it immensely. They spent about three hours checking fences before heading back to the ranch.

It was late in the day when they returned. They saw a lone rider on his horse waiting for them. It was one of their neighbors, Ted Matthews.

"Walt, thank God you're here. I have some bad news."

"What is it, Ted?" Walt asked.

Ted Matthews was visibly upset. He said, "We were taking a herd to Abilene and we found where your herd was rustled. Your foreman Cal was still alive. I'm sorry Walt, but your wife and four hands were all shot dead. Two of my men are bringing the bodies in a wagon. I have them all wrapped up in blankets. The rustlers not only shot them, they ran the herd over them too. It wasn't a pleasant sight." He went on, "I suggest that you leave them tied up in their blankets for burial."

Walt got down off his horse and then helped Orin dismount. Orin was sobbing uncontrollably. Walt held him in his arms for a moment and then led him into the ranch house.

He said, "Lie down for awhile Orin; I have to talk to this man a bit more."

Walt went outside just as the wagon arrived with the bodies. He went to the bunk house and found two of the hands resting there. Walt woke the men and brought them outside. Together they lifted the bodies out of the wagon and placed them on the ground.

When they finished, Walt thanked Ted Matthews for all that he had done.

Matthews said, "When my herd gets to Abilene my foreman is going to see the sheriff and tell him what happened. They will probably raise a posse and go after the rustlers. A few of my men want to go with them."

Walt thanked him again and asked where it had happened and what direction they were heading. When he had the information he shook Matthews hand and thanked him again. After Ted left, Walt gathered his men together and asked them to take lanterns up to a small knoll in back of the ranch. He said, "We'll bury them all there."

They had several caskets out in the barn. There had been an epidemic of some kind a few years earlier and one of the hands had made many caskets. Thankfully, they hadn't needed all of them back then. The men loaded the bodies in the caskets and put them on a flat work wagon and then rode out to the burial place. They dug four graves on one side of the knoll for the men. Walt dug one grave for Myra on the other side of the knoll. After all of the bodies were buried, Walt told the men he was leaving for a few days. The men protested. They wanted to ride along with him.

Walt said, "I need you to guard my land, my cattle, and most of all, my son. I have work to do and I have to get started now. Jim, you will be acting foreman until Cal gets back on his feet. Take good care of things for me, I'm counting on you."

Walt went out to the barn and collected his rifle, three boxes of shells, and a handgun that he jammed into his belt. He also took down an old .50 caliber buffalo rifle that had been hanging over the inside of the barn door. He filled his pockets with shells for the buffalo rifle, saddled his horse and rode off.

It was dark by then but he knew where he was going to be at sunup. He should be able to track them down from there.

CHAPTER TWO

Five days later Walt knew he was being followed. He kept on the trail and just before sundown he stopped to make camp. He was resting by the campfire when he heard something. He said, "Mister I don't know who you are but unless you show yourself I'm going to start shooting in your direction. I should be able to hit you."

An Indian stepped out of the shadows. Walt knew him.

"Running Horse is that you?"

"Yes Sanger, it is me," he replied.

"Well what are you following me for?!"

"My chief, Red Cloud, commanded me to follow and protect you.

We know what has happened. You have been good to our people, and like a brother to us."

Red Cloud was a White Mountain Apache. His people had served as scouts with General Crook. They were supposed to be on a reservation but as it happened the reservation was located on their former lands. Walt gave them a few steer when their hunting wasn't too good. Myra was also a help to them as well. Walt and Myra both had good relations with the tribe and the tribe especially adored her.

Running Horse said, "Rest for two hours and then we will be on our way. I know where they are keeping your cattle."

Walt's heart leaped in his chest. He said, "I want my cattle but most of all I want the men who killed my wife."

Running Horse nodded and lay down near the small campfire he had made. Two hours later they were on their way.

Walt said, "I want to reach them before the Posse does."

Running Horse smiled. He thought to himself, "Sanger would make a good Apache."

By mid afternoon they came across the track of many cattle.

Walt said, "My neighbor claims the rustlers headed west so let's be on our way."

The Indian smiled and said, "No my friend, we will head northwest. We aren't the only ones tracking this herd. Two of my fellow braves are following them; they are leaving signs for me to follow. We can track faster now."

He headed off at a gallop. Walt followed closely. He couldn't detect any of the signs but he knew Running Horse could see them. After an hour of hard riding they stopped.

Running Horse said, "Do you see those mountains ahead of you? There is a trail that we will follow. There is a valley in the middle of that range that the cattle are grazing on."

Walt was amazed but didn't question him at all. When they finally reached the mountain range they dismounted and climbed to a place where they could view the valley without being seen. There were hundreds of cattle bottled up in the valley. They were grazing on the lush grass there.

Walt thought, "Mine aren't the only cattle here."

The mountains ringed the valley on all sides with only a few openings. The largest one was where the rustlers brought the cattle in.

One of Running Horse's braves rode up. He spoke briefly with Running Horse and then rode back to his post near the large opening of the valley.

Running Horse rode up to Walt and said, "There are about ten men guarding the cattle. There was another one but he rode off earlier.

They look like they are going to change the brands on the cattle. Do you think they will do this at night?"

Walt thought for a moment and said, "It's hard enough to brand in the daylight. I don't think they'll do it tonight."

Walt asked how many ways there were out of the valley.

Running Horse answered, "There are three ways to ride out of the valley but a man on foot can climb out anywhere."

Walt asked him to take one of the braves and guard the large opening.

"I just want you to keep them in the valley. I don't want you or your braves to be tried for killing a white man – that's my job."

Walt told Running Horse to station the other brave at the second opening and he would take the third.

Walt said, "I'll start shooting at first light when they start to change the brands."

He was just settling in for a quick nap when he noticed the rustlers piling logs for a fire. It was too far away for effective shooting so he traded places with the second Indian brave. He settled in for a nap.

CHAPTER THREE

Walt awoke suddenly and sat up. He looked into the valley, it was still dark but you could see daylight coming in the distance. Men were moving around in the camp. They started their cook fires and also started the fire where the branding would take place. Walt moved to where he had a commanding view of the valley. He carefully loaded the buffalo gun and the carbine. His handgun was cleaned and loaded the night before.

Walt watched as the rustlers cleaned their utensils with sand and grass. The men went over to the log fire. It was ready. They put their branding irons into the fire and waited.

When the irons were glowing red they upended one of the cows and proceeded to brand over the old brand. The cow was bawling as they released it. Two men brought the next cow to the fire and threw it down. The rustler leaned over to get the branding iron. As the rustler's hand closed over the handle, Walt fired the buffalo gun. The rustler was thrown into the fire. Sparks and embers covered the other two men and the cow.

They released the cow and clawed for their side arms. Walt lay down the buffalo gun and reached for his carbine. He fired twice and both men went down. "That's three", he muttered to himself. The Indians continued to open fire on the remaining rustlers. They kept them back from the escape openings and under Walt's rifle.

The rustlers hollered out "We're surrounded, every man for himself!"

Walt slowly picked them off one by one. Within an hour he had all of them except one.

One of the braves came running up to him and said, "Sanger, there is a large party of white men coming, we must leave."

Walt agreed, "It's probably the posse from Abilene. I don't want you braves to be found here. I'll follow you shortly."

Walt mounted his horse and went to the large opening to the valley. He emptied his rifle into the ground in front of the cattle. They started to stampede back and forth inside the valley. He couldn't see the last rustler but he was hoping the stampede would get him. He turned and headed swiftly out of the mountain range. He saw the cloud of dirt from the posse bearing down on the hideout. "There must be fifty people," he thought.

CHAPTER FOUR

Walt didn't see the last rustler leave the range after him. He was thinking of his wife and son. He cried bitterly for a few minutes and then galloped for home.

The surviving rustler was following Walt's trail. His name was Matt Rydell. He was a killer and rustler and he was damn mad. He had to dive into a crevice in the mountain to keep from being trampled. He saw the posse coming so he decided to follow the rifleman's tracks. "I'll put a bullet in him for every man that I lost," he thought to himself.

Walt rode through the night, not hard riding but steady. He rested a few hours and then started off again. The next morning he knew the horse had needed a good night's rest more than he did. He made camp early and decided to wake up early in the morning. He could make home by mid-day. He didn't make a fire, he just rolled up in his blanket and within minutes was sound asleep.

Matt Rydell rode along in the evening light. He stopped, took out a telescope and surveyed the surrounding territory. "Damn," he thought, "where is he? He has to be bedded down somewhere." He decided to camp near a few big boulders. They would provide shelter from the wind and also hide a small fire.

Walt was abruptly awakened by something. He listened...nothing. But what woke him up? He sat up and unwound the blanket. Standing up he cupped his hands to his eyes Indian style and scanned the horizon. He passed over the place where the big boulders were. He scanned over them again, closely. There was a flicker of light reflecting on one of the boulders. Someone's there and they have a small fire. It might be the last rustler or it could be a traveler who just happened to camp near him. He thought, "I can't chance it."

He broke camp. He tried to eliminate any trace of the campsite and then he saddled up his horse and turned for home.

Matt Rydell woke up from a deep sleep. Daybreak was almost here. He saw that the fire had gotten out of control for a while and burned some dry grass near one of the boulders. He worried about it for a while, broke camp, and rode off. At daylight he could see the rifleman's trail and quickly followed it to the rifleman's campsite. Matt was hoping to catch him in his blanket roll. All he found was where the man had made camp. Looking back along the trail he could see the boulders where he had made camp and cursed. The fire must have been seen by the rifleman. "Damn." He whirled his horse around and started looking for the rifleman's trail. Once he found it he galloped off after him.

Rydell rode until the sun was high overhead. He found a high place where he could scan the trail ahead. He saw a small plume of dust in the distance. "I got you now, boy, I got you now," he said again. He mounted up and started in pursuit.

CHAPTER FIVE

Orin Sanger missed his ma and pa. He knew his mother was dead and buried. He put fresh flowers on her grave every day. He didn't know where his pa was. He wanted to follow him but he was not a good tracker yet. And if he would have he'd probably have gotten lost and never seen him again. He did follow the trail for a little while but he could see his pa had been moving fast and had probably caught up to the rustlers already.

Each day since Pa had left he followed his tracks to a small knoll overlooking the trail. He brought his rifle with him. Orin hadn't wanted the rifle at first but his pa told him every rancher has an obligation to his family and cattle to protect them from harm. Pa had taught him well. Orin was nine and a half years-old and could already shoot as well as some of the ranch hands. Pa was the best rifleman in the world, he thought beaming.

Orin started to turn off the knoll where he spotted dust on the trail He smiled, "That's got to be Pa."

He looked past the swirling dust and saw more dust farther back on the trail. It was moving faster than Pa. Orin got down from his horse and climbed to his favorite looking post. He loaded the rifle and waited. Walt heard the shot before the bullet struck. It came from a long way off. He fell off his horse and felt his shoulder. It was wet with blood. "I should have stayed and finished him off," he thought. He heard the rider approach. He tried to reach the handgun in his belt but was too weak to do it.

He heard a voice say, "Well boy, you must be the one that ruined a very good business of mine and my partner's."

He saw the blood on Walt's shoulder and laughed, "I really didn't know if I could make that shot or not. I guess I'm better than I thought I was."

Matt Rydell dismounted and came over to Walt, "I could take your horse and let you bleed to death on the trail, but I want the satisfaction of knowing that I killed you. I'm going to put a bullet in your heart while you are looking at me."

He drew his handgun and stood over Walt, "Say goodbye boy, here you go." He pulled back the hammer.

Walt looked skyward and thought, "I'm sorry Orin, I tried."

He heard a grunt and looked at the rustler. A big red rose blossomed out of the side of his head and he fell over Walt's body. He thought he heard something and then realized it was someone calling. It sounded like Orin. He passed out.

When Walt opened his eyes again Orin was there. He had pushed the rustler off him and was pressing his shirt against Walt's wound to stop the bleeding.

Orin wiped Walt's face and talked to him, he was crying, "I had to shoot him Pa, he was going to shoot you."

"I know son, I know that you feel bad but think about this. The man you shot helped kill your mother and four of our ranch hands. That should help ease your pain."

"You're right, Pa," Orin said, "He was a snake and now I feel better."

Orin helped his father up on his horse and then mounted his own horse.

"What are we going to do about the rustler, Pa?"

"I'll have a few of the hands come back and bury him and turn his horse loose. Let's go," said Walt.

When they arrived at the ranch his foreman Cal was waiting for them. He apologized for not protecting Myra better than he had.

"I was grazed with the first shot and knocked out of my saddle. The chuck wagon must have protected me from the stampede. I don't remember anymore than that, I'm so sorry Walt."

"I know old friend, you couldn't have done any more than you did. I tracked them down, I got nine of them. The last one trailed me and almost got me. He shot me off my horse and was about to finish me off when Orin drilled him in the head. I'd like you to take a few men and go back down the trail and bury him and turn his horse loose."

"Will do boss, but let's get that bullet out of you first before the sheriff comes."

Walt said, "I don't want the sheriff to know that it was me that got those rustlers. I fell off my horse and I'm recuperating. Pass the word."

Cal called Orin over and said, "When I pull the bullet out, pour some of my whiskey on the wound. It will kill any bugs in there."

Orin nodded and did as he was told. His father winced in agony as the whiskey entered his flesh. Tears streamed down Orin's cheeks as he kept pouring whiskey into the wound.

Cal said, "Alright boy that's enough. I don't want to have to go to town to get another bottle."

He finished bandaging the wound and left to talk to the ranch hands.

Cal and two of the hands went back along the trail to the spot that Walt had described where the shooting took place. They found the rustler and started digging his grave. Cal started to roll the body into a blanket when he suddenly stopped and told the hands there would be no need for a grave.

Cal said "I know this hard case and I know who he works for."

They rolled the rustler in the blanket and tied him to his horse. They all mounted and were riding out past the boundaries to the ranch.

Cal said, "Pete you're pretty good with a gun so I want you to back me up. Whitey you lay back a bit and cover us with your rifle. I'm sure there's going to be some shooting."

They rode on and finally entered the Matthews's range and headed for the ranch house. Luke Rydell saw them and hollered for Ted Matthews.

"Hey boss we got company."

Ted Matthews came out to the porch to greet the visitors. "It's okay Luke, it's just some of our neighbors from the Sanger ranch, ease off."

Luke put his gun back in its holster.

Matthews said, "Howdy Cal what can I do for you?"

"Well sir," Cal said, "We had a heap of trouble a while back as you know. All of the rustlers are dead. This here is the last of them."

He untied the blanket and let the body roll out on the ground. Luke Rydell let out a groan as he saw his dead brother lying on the ground.

"Why did you bring him here?" Matthews said after cautioning Luke with a wave of his hand.

"Well Mr. Matthews I recognized this one. I was in the saloon last year in the back room when this Jasper and the one on the porch with you first hired on with you. I saw the handshaking and the smiles when you closed the deal. I reckon we know who's behind all the rustling that's been going on."

Cal looked at Luke Rydell and said, "Keep your hands where I can see them. If one hand leaves my sight I'll kill you on the spot."

Luke said, "Who is this Mr. Matthews?"

Matthews said, "It's Cal Rankin I'm sure you've heard of him."

"You mean this old coot is Cal Rankin the gunfighter?!"

"Yes, and I'd do what he says if I were you."

"Well Rankin, I'm Luke Rydell have you heard of me?"

Cal acknowledged, "Yes, you are a back-shooting killer and a thief. I've heard of you."

Rydell said, "Mr. Matthews, I think we can take them if you have a mind to."

"Wait," Matthews said.

"Cal, what are you going to do?"

"Well Matthews," Cal said, "When you killed Myra Sanger you got the whole territory after your head. You have two choices. Come with me to the sheriff's office and later be hanged or die now drawing on me, your choice. Make it now."

Matthews nodded at Rydell and they both drew at the same time. As it always has been in the past, Cal's gun came up blazing first. The first bullet took Rydell in the heart. The next two blew Matthews off the porch. Well," Cal thought, "That should end the rustling for a while."

Cal and Pete went into the ranch house and searched for anything to do with the cattle rustling operation. Later Cal, Pete, and Whitey loaded the three bodies onto a wagon that was in the barn. The three then rode off to the Sanger ranch.

CHAPTER SIX

Orin called to his father "Pa, some men are coming. It looks like they're driving our cattle home."

The sheriff was with them. He rode up to the house. Walt was sitting on the porch.

"Walt I think we got all of your cattle here. The other ranchers culled out theirs. These were all that was left. There's about a hundred head."

Walt said, "That's just about the amount we sent to market. Thanks a lot sheriff and thank all of the men for me, will you?"

"I surely will, Walt. How are you feeling? I'm truly sorry for your loss."

"I thank you kindly sheriff. I'm doing fine. I fell off my horse the other day I'm still hurting a bit from that."

The sheriff went on, "We found nine bodies in the canyon. The cattle stampeded and made a mess of them. They were all shot too. The official word I put out was that they were all killed in the stampede. I thought you would like to know that. We buried them on the spot, no markers."

"Thanks again sheriff, I appreciate that."

Cal and the two ranch hands rode up just as the sheriff was ready to leave.

"Hold on sheriff," Cal said, "I want you to hear this."

Cal related the story about going to the Matthews' ranch and the subsequent gunfight. He produced papers found in the ranch house relating to the rustling operation.

"Matthews was hired to scare off the ranch owners in the valley so a big conglomerate could own it all. It's right here in Matthews's own handwriting along with the letters he received."

The sheriff said, "Don't that beat all, I never would have suspected Ted Matthews."

The sheriff turned to Cal and said, "Cal you and your two friends are going to have to return with me to settle another matter."

"What's that sheriff?"

"Well Cal, there's a reward for the Rydell brothers. I've got some posters of them back at the office. We'll take the wagon and bodies up to Boot Hill and bury them. Come to town in the next day or two and I'll try to have your reward for you."

Cal, Pete, and Whitey left with a big smile on their faces. They left to take the cattle out to the range to graze. Walt Sanger called Orin over to his side. Orin had a strange look on his face and Walt knew why.

Walt said, "I know in the past I told you about lying. I want you to remember what I told the sheriff. I told him I fell off my horse and actually that's true. I just left out the fact that a bullet caused me to fall. That wasn't a lie, was it?"

Orin laughed, "No Pa, you told him the truth."

They sat on the porch until the sheriff and the men rode out of sight. "Orin it's important that you realize that the sheriff knows exactly what happened and he knows justice was served."

"We are going to miss your mother Orin. She was the heart and soul of our ranch. Maybe together we can honor her memory by building the ranch as a monument to her."

They went into the house to make plans.

That night Cal rode up to the house and called for Walt. They went for a walk behind the barn where no one could see or hear them.

"Walt, I turned over all of the papers to the sheriff. There's no doubt that Matthews and the people he worked for are guilty as sin. I neglected to tell the sheriff about the money box I found. Pete and Whitey don't know about it either. I want you to have it." He went on, "I know it can't come anywhere near replacing your loss and the grief you have now, but I have a few ideas on how you can use the money. The Matthews ranch borders on your land. You can make a bid on it. I'm sure the sheriff and the judge will allow you to buy it. Think of it as a legacy to Myra and a better future for Orin."

Cal went to the barn and retrieved the box that he had put there earlier.

Walt accepted the box and said, "Old friend you have helped me so much in the past. I don't know how to repay you."

"Walt, you and Myra and Orin are the only family that I can remember. Just keep a place for me at the chuck wagon that's all I want."

They both broke into laughter and walked back to the ranch. Two weeks later Walt Sanger bought the Matthews ranch.

CHAPTER SEVEN

Orin Sanger was one day shy of seventeen years-old. He was almost six foot tall and still growing. Being a ranch hand for his father agreed with him. He weighed in at one hundred and seventy-five pounds of hard muscle. Finishing his chores in the barn, Orin called to his dog and then closed and latched the barn door. As he started for the house, the dog growled and began to bark. Orin looked in all directions but couldn't see anything. He walked over to the corral and climbed up on the top rail. He saw dust being raised on the trail and waited until he could make out what it was. He jumped down from the fence and ran to the house.

He called out, "Pa, four riders coming in pretty fast!"

Walt Sanger came out on the porch. He took one look at the advancing riders and then turned to his son. His ranch hands and Cal were all on a cattle drive. The two were alone.

"Orin, we already talked about this and you know what to do. Get in the barn and lock it from inside. Stay put, no matter what happens, understand?"

Orin said, "Yes, Pa," and ran for the barn. After locking the barn door, he went to the front wall and got down his rifle, loaded it and set it by the gun hole near the barn door. He looked out and saw that Pa had gotten his shotgun and was holding it on his lap.

Orin stared at the back stall as if trying to make up his mind about something. Yep, Pa was going to need him more than ever today. He might as well find out now. He went quickly to the back stall, pushed away the straw and lifted out two floorboards. He very carefully took out a package wrapped in an old blanket and oil skin paper. In a matter of moments he opened the package and gazed lovingly at the year-old Colt .44 six-shooter that was inside. It was his given to him on his sixteenth birthday by a special friend.

He climbed the ladder to the hayloft and retrieved his gun belt and holster and made his way back down. As soon as his feet touched the ground again he adjusted the belt and tied down the holster. He slid the colt forty-four in the holster for a moment. He quickly drew the colt and put it back in the holster. He did it several times. He checked to make sure it was fully loaded and settled it in the holster again. He was ready.

Orin thought of his best friend Cal Rankin. He was almost nine years-old when Cal came to work for his pa. They knew each other from way back and Pa was sure glad to see him again. He said he was tired of the life he had been leading and wanted to settle down. Pa hired him on the spot and made him foreman of the ranch. Cal was a natural with the men and he soon took over most of the duties of running the ranch. He and Orin took a liking to each other, right off.

One afternoon when Pa was in town, Orin heard some shooting and went to investigate. Cal and a few of the hands were having a quick draw and shoot contest. Cal won hands down each time. Orin never expected anyone could draw that fast. After the contest was over and Cal and Orin were alone, Orin asked Cal if he would teach him to quick draw and shoot.

Cal agreed, "Yes but it has to be a secret from your pa."

Pa was an expert with a rifle but he never carried a hand gun. Cal let Orin know that if his pa knew about this he would probably fire him. They both promised they wouldn't tell Pa. Then they spit on their hands and shook on it. That was almost eight years ago.

Orin remembered the early days of practice with the frame and handle from an old colt. Hour after hour each day, every day, every free moment, he practiced. He was almost thirteen when he started using live ammunition on targets.

Cal told him at that time he was faster than most of the ranch hands and gunslingers in the area. As Orin grew, it became a labor of love. He recalled on his sixteenth birthday when Cal gave him his new Colt 44. He had just tied down the holster and turned toward Cal. Orin called out,

"Draw." Cal was reaching for his own colt and found himself looking down the muzzle of Orin's new gun.

Cal could hardly believe it. When had the kid gotten so fast? He didn't even see the draw. A blink of an eye and there was the muzzle in his face. Cal tried to mask the fear in his eyes and mumbled about his own clumsiness. Then he got serious and told Orin that he had never seen a faster draw from anyone before.

He said, "You have a gift that no other man has. You can and will be the fastest shooter in the west. Use this skill wisely."

He added, "Remember, don't ever let on to your pa that I taught you how to draw and shoot."

Orin said, "Don't worry Cal." They promised, spit, and shook on it.

"Remember it's our sacred oath."

Now Orin's thoughts about how Pa would react to his skill with the Colt brought him back to the present. He was going to be shocked.

Orin heard the horses come into the yard and put his face up to the gun hole. Four men rode in to the yard. The first man was Major Stanton, the owner of the biggest ranch in the valley. He was followed by his foreman Mark Sadler and two strangers that he had never seen before. The two strangers had their holsters tied down. "They must be the two enforcers that Pa and I heard of," thought Orin.

Walt Sanger walked over to the fence and laid his shotgun over the second rail, covering all of the riders effectively at the same time.

Major Stanton said, "You aren't very neighborly Sanger, we just want to talk."

Walt Sanger said, "Nothing to talk about Major, I told you in town my spread is not for sale at any price. That still goes." The Major shook his head and said, "Sanger, I need the water and grazing land you have on your ranch. I offered a good price for it, why don't you take it?"

"My wife is buried on this ranch and my son's roots are here, that's reason enough. We are not going to leave."

One of the strangers spoke up, "Where is that cub of yours Sanger? I hear he's all growed up."

Walt said, "He's in town getting supplies." The Major piped up again, "Sanger, I mean to have this ranch one way or another."

Before Walt could answer the barn door burst open and Orin came out to face the horsemen. He looked at the Major and said,

"Mr. Stanton, I won't have you or anyone else threatening my pa that way. You have his answer now get out and take your gun hands with you."

Walt Sanger was struck dumb. This wasn't his young son. This was a stranger to him. He noticed the expertly tied down holster and the gleam of the well cared for colt forty-four. What he noticed most was the self-assured way that he handled himself.

Orin called out "Don't do it mister, swing your leg back up over your horse."

The stranger dismounted and said, "Boy, you need some manners taught to you." He went on, "You don't even know who I am and you're trying to tell me what to do. Do you know what my name is?"

Orin shook his head no.

"Well its Jack Norton, ever hear of me?"

Orin shook his head again.

"Boy, I happen to be the fastest gun in these parts."

Orin said, "I don't think so."

"Boy," Jack Norton said, "you ever kill a man in a gunfight?"

"You'll be the first." Orin replied.

Norton whistled, "Now don't you beat all."

Orin said, "Yes."

Norton looked a little uneasy and then covered it by saying, "I'm going to let you draw first boy. Get on with it and make sure your first shot counts, don't just wound me."

Orin said, "Mister, if I draw this colt you will be dead. I don't shoot to wound."

Walt Sanger recalled Cal saying that some years back. He thought, damn, Cal taught Orin how to draw and shoot right under my nose. He probably bought him the gun too. Walt slowly turned and aimed the shot gun at Major Stanton and his foreman and thought, "If they try to get into the action I'll take them both out."

Orin said, "Mr. Stanton, will you please count to three? When you reach three we'll have at it, but first tell your other gunsel to put his hands on his pommel or I'll blow him out of the saddle."

The man quickly put his hands on the pommel of his saddle.

"All right Mr. Stanton, start counting."

The Major began, "One…two…three." Norton clawed for his gun. It was almost free of his holster when he heard two shots. He felt one hammer into his chest and he fell back as his partner was blown from his saddle. His eyes glazed over and then he was gone.

The Major stared at Orin and said, "Young man you are going to regret this."

Orin laughed and said, "Stanton, tell your foreman to load this trash on their horses and get out of here. I want all weapons including yours in a pile by the fence."

The Major's face was red with anger.

"Young man," he said, "show me the respect I deserve and call me Major Stanton."

Orin said, "You aren't in the army anymore Stanton, and your band of cutthroats is down by two. Now shuck those gun belts and do what I said!"

Stanton nodded to his foreman and they dropped their gun belts and rifles on the ground. The foreman loaded the bodies on their horses and started off.

Major Stanton turned to leave when Orin stopped him, "I'll have a word with you Stanton."

They were well out of earshot of Walt and the foreman. He walked up to the horse and looked into his eyes.

"Give me your attention Major." The major, quite surprised, said, "Yes."

"I didn't want my pa to hear me. I know the sheriff is going to get a different story about what happened here today, so I aim to move on and leave the territory so that I don't cause my pa any trouble. I just want you to listen carefully about what I'm saying. If my pa dies early or something happens that makes him lose his ranch, I'll be back. If my pa dies because of your trickery or wrong doing, I'll kill every living thing on your ranch. This means your cattle, your ranch hands, your family, and you. I'll save you for last to witness all of it. I'll burn your ranch, shoot you and throw you in the fire. Believe me I will do it. Now get out of here and leave my pa alone."

The major stared at him and felt the tremors of fear engulfing him. He rode ahead to join his foreman. They left the ranch at a gallop.

Orin walked up to his father, "I'm sorry, Pa, I didn't mean to cause you any trouble, I'll be moving on in a little while."

Walt hugged his son and said, "I had hoped that you could grow up and not have to do what you just did. It wasn't your fault, you gave them every chance. I was and still am, proud of you son. I'll get things ready for you while you go say goodbye to your mother."

Walt fixed up his son's saddlebags and blanket roll. He went into the barn and saddled his favorite horse. Everything was ready when Orin returned from the grave site.

"Pa, I can't take Ole Satan, he's your favorite."

"I know son but he will sure eat up the miles for you. Take him with my blessings."

Walt handed him a small sack of money. This is your wages for the past six months. You've earned it."

Orin put the money in his shirt pocket. He hugged his father one more time and then swung up into the saddle. He rode off down the road, looked back once, saw his pa still waving. He waved back, turned around and headed west.

Orin was ten miles down the road before the enormity of what had happened, hit him. He sagged in the saddle. I'm almost seventeen years- old and I have already killed three men and threatened another with great bodily harm. He wondered when he would be able to see his pa again. The tears flowed down his cheeks.

CHAPTER EIGHT

Orin headed up into the territory of New Mexico. He had been there a few times with Pa but wasn't familiar with anything that he saw now. He shaded his eyes and stood up in his stirrups for a better view. He saw something in the distance and his heart leaped in his chest. It was a huge rock formation that Orin and his pa had named St. Peter's Gate. It was almost one hundred feet high and about two hundred and fifty feet around. Pa had calculated the size of the rock formation and wasn't too far off. It was loaded with jutting rocks and crevices that could be used for climbing. They climbed it once and the view was breathtaking.

Orin headed for the formation to see if anything had changed. He was part way around it when he heard someone shouting and cursing.

He continued around the rock formation and came upon a terrible sight. There were four men. One man was holding the reins of the horses for the other three men. The three men were busy terrorizing a young Indian. Two of them were holding him down while the third man was trying to carve something on his chest. The young Indian didn't even whimper. He stared with hatred at the white men who were torturing him.

At the sound of Orin's horse the four men looked over at him and one hollered, "Boy don't you come riding in quiet like that. We could have shot you!"

Orin said, "Let the boy go and stand away from him."

The man replied, "Boy when I finish carving my name on him, you can have him."

"No more talk, let him go or I'll shoot you off of him."

One of the men went for his gun. Then all hell broke loose. Orin drew and fired four times. The three men with the Indian boy were dead. The fourth man had his hands up high.

He said, "It ain't my fight boy, I didn't know what they were going to do with the Indian. Major Stanton wouldn't have liked it either."

Orin groaned, "Stanton again."

He motioned for the man to drop his gun belt. He checked the condition of the young Indian. He didn't look good. He had been beaten badly first, before he was tortured.

He called the man over again, "Do you know how to build a travois?"

The man answered, "Yes."

Orin said, "Get started. It has to hold three bodies. He ministered to the Indian while the man worked. He tended to the wounds and gave him his canteen for a long drink of water.

When the man finished, they loaded the three bodies on the travois. Orin allowed him one extra horse.

Orin announced, "By the time you deliver these men back to the major, I'll be long gone. I'll take their guns and ammunition plus the two extra horses. You can have their money and personal property with one handgun."

The man thanked him and as he turned to go said, "Get the Indian to those mountains yonder, his people are there."

Orin watched the two horses and the travois until they were out of sight.

He turned to the Indian boy, "Do you understand my language?" The Indian just stared at him.

"Please I'm just trying to help you."

The boy smiled and said, "Yes."

"Can you ride or do you want me to build a travois?"

The boy laughed and said, "Apaches are men, we ride the horse."

Orin helped him mount up and tied him to the saddle so he wouldn't fall off. He packed all the guns and ammunition on the extra horse and gathering up the reins of all the horses, rode off to the mountains.

He lost a half day of traveling time getting the Indian boy to the mountains. He stopped at the foothills and looked around. Orin sensed someone nearby but couldn't see anyone. He was looking at the mountains for some kind of clue to where the Indian camp was. He felt a sharp pain at the back of his head and fell off his horse. He could hear shouts of the Indians and then he heard the young Indian cry out, just as he passed out.

When Orin awoke, he was lying by a fire in some kind of tent. A young Indian girl was putting cool wet cloths on his head. She smiled at him, got up, and went outside. In a few minutes an Indian walked into the tent and sat beside him.

"My son has told me what you did for him. I would like to know why you helped him against your own kind."

Orin smiled and said, "There is only mankind. Your son was a young man like me. The others were the bad side of mankind. They deserved what they got."

The Indian said, "Your answer shows wisdom beyond your years. My people have read the signs, will they come looking for you."

Orin answered, "Yes they will come, but I will not be here and make trouble for you."

"You will stay until you are rested for travel. We will hide you if anyone comes."

Three days later, Orin and the Indian boy were talking when a scout came running in shouting, "They are coming! Twenty riders, and a man wearing a badge is leading them."

An older Indian came up to them and said, "Get all of your belongings you two have and follow me."

Orin loaded all of the weapons that he had taken from the men he had shot, on the extra pack horse. He jumped into the saddle. Ole Satan galloped after the two Indians.

They rode over half a day and came upon a large mountain range. The older Indian rode up to Orin and said, "You are going to see what no other white man has seen. I was going to cover your eyes but I feel that I can trust you now. Watch this."

He spoke to the young Indian boy and he rode off at a gallop. He didn't ride around the base of the mountain in front of him. He rode right at it. He suddenly disappeared. Orin rode with his mouth wide open. The older Indian laughed.

He said, "Come."

They rode up to the mountain. There was a lot of scrub brush around the base of the mountain. The Indian dismounted and Orin did the same. The Indian pushed aside some of the brush and revealed a cave. The entrance was large enough to allow their horses to walk into.

After the horses were all in, the Indian, with the help of Orin, pulled the brush back over the entrance again. Orin could see light in the distance. They walked about two hundred feet on a winding trail through the mountain and came out to a valley inside the mountain range. There was a river running through the valley and Indian teepees were set up on both sides of the river. Small children were playing in the river. Their mothers were keeping a watchful eye on them. Orin was amazed. There were vegetables and gardens growing everywhere. There were a few deer hanging from tree branches waiting to be skinned.

They rode up to the largest teepee in the valley. The young Indian was talking to a man of indeterminate age. The young Indian was pointing his finger at Orin and was smiling. The Indian waved his hand at the boy and he immediately became quiet.

The man spoke to Orin, "Come stand beside me."

Orin dismounted and walked over to the Indian.

"I have heard wonderful things about you from my nephew. I am called Red Fox. My brother is chief of our tribe. Your father is well known to us, he is a good man and now you also are a good man. You will stay with us until it is safe for you to leave."

Orin thanked him. Orin and the young Indian were given a tent next to Red Fox's tent. It was an honor, the boy explained.

Orin and the boy unloaded all of their gear. Orin presented Red Fox with a fine rifle and pistol. He gave White Fox a gun belt with a holstered gun.

"I will teach you to shoot while I am here."

White Fox was impressed with Orin's quick draw.

"Will I be able to do that?" he asked.

Orin said, "If I stay here long enough you will."

The next morning, Red Fox summoned Orin to his tent. They sat across from each other.

Red Fox began to speak, "I am known all over this country, not just by the Red man but also by all of the whites. I am a tracker and reader of signs of nature. I do not boast. What I say is true. I teach members of other tribes how to read the signs in nature. They send their young men to me that I may school them in the ways of men and animals." Red Fox continued, "I was deeply honored by your great gift of the rifle and handgun. I thought a long time on what gift I could give you that was worthy of yours. If you agree to spend more time with us here in the valley, I will teach you along with my nephew White Fox all that I have learned about tracking and reading the signs of nature."

Orin was overwhelmed by Red Fox and his gift. He knew that he should be moving on but the knowledge that he would gain by staying longer, won out.

"Red Fox I accept your gift with joy in my heart."

"You already think and talk like an Indian, now we will teach you all of our ways. We begin tomorrow."

SIX MONTHS LATER...

Orin and White Fox were being tested. They were to follow a trail laid out by older members of the tribe. They had made their way outside of the valley now. They became separated and started off on trails out of sight of each other. There were things to pick up along the trail to show that they didn't take any shortcuts along the way. The trails would end at an old abandoned water hole.

Four hours later, Orin had collected all of his items from the trail. He shaded his eyes and looked all around the water hole. White Fox was nowhere to be seen. He sat behind a small knoll and waited. An hour later he spied White Fox hobbling down the trail to the water hole. He waited until White Fox reached it and then ran down the trail to join him. White Fox was elated that he had won.

One of the members of the tribe rode up with their horses. They raced back to the valley. The tribe had a victory celebration for White Fox. He was beaming. He explained to everyone how he had twisted his ankle sliding down a culvert but he kept on and won the race.

While the celebration was going on, Red Fox summoned Orin to his tent again.

"What you did today was good. White Fox will never know that you had beaten him; you have given him great pride. You and I know that you have proven to be a better student than anyone else in the valley. You learn faster and have a greater understanding of the Mother Earth that surrounds us. I am proud to know you, Orin Sanger." He continued, "As of today I will make it known to all that you are my adopted nephew and should be treated with the respect that goes with the title. Are you well with this?"

Orin sat with his mouth open and now closed it and with a big smile said, "I am deeply honored, Uncle."

Red Fox said, "You and my other nephew will help train the new students in our humble school." They smiled at each other and went to join the celebration.

TWO YEARS LATER...

Orin got up and went to the river to bathe. He sat in the river and let the water wash away the sweat of sleep from him. He was naked except for his breech cloth. His headband kept his long hair in place. He saw his reflection in the water. He looked more like an Indian than half the tribe members.

Today he was going to continue teaching White Fox and some select members to quick draw and shoot. White Fox was progressing nicely. In fact he was quite fast. He was no match for Orin but he could hold his own with most of the rowdies he had seen.

Orin was still practicing every day. He could draw and shoot with either hand. He put on an exhibition for his Uncle and his friends. They marveled at his speed and accuracy. White Fox was an expert with the bow and arrow. He had been teaching Orin for the last two years. He had learned his lessons well. Red Fox had the best bow maker in the tribe make a custom bow and arrows for Orin. He and White Fox were a formidable pair. They challenged all comers to test their skill, and won every time.

One day while cleaning their weapons a rider came up and went immediately to Red Fox. He spoke for a few moments and left. Red Fox waved Orin and White Fox to his side.

He told them, "A white man was seen with the Indians and a posse is being formed to hunt him down." Red Fox went on, "It is time for you to leave, my nephew. You will be greatly missed."

He took an amulet from around his neck and placed it around Orin's neck. "Show this to any of the people and you will be granted safe passage," he said.

White Fox helped Orin with his saddlebags and blanket roll. "You are my brother Orin Sanger."

"And you are mine," Orin said.

He swung up onto ole Satan, waved at everyone, and rode off.

Orin rode hard the first day. He rode until dark. He didn't light a fire because it would be like a beacon for any pursuers to hone in on. He and Ole Satan bedded down for the night. The next morning he found the tracks of a cattle drive. They were heading southwest. He followed them for a day and then headed northwest again. He enjoyed the scenery. He stopped to hunt and shot a small deer with the bow and arrow. Orin roasted the meat over a small fire and smoked some strips of venison the way the Indians had taught him. His thoughts drifted back to his father.

CHAPTER NINE

Red Fox sent his braves to check on his father once in a while so he knew he was alright. He missed him terribly. He also missed Red Fox and his nephew White Fox. Orin slept that night with a full stomach.

When he woke up in the morning he headed due west. Two days later he entered Arizona territory. Someone had erected a crude sign:

'South to Tucson – north to Fort Defiance.'

Orin decided to travel due west. The big town and the fort may have a wanted poster on him. He traveled for a few hours and then heard two shots ring out. He stopped and listened. The valleys and canyons echoed the shots and he couldn't determine which direction they came from. It could have been a hunter.

He rode on slowly. An hour later he saw something on the trail in front of him. He took his telescope from his saddlebag and scanned the trail. Someone was laying on the trail. He urged Ole Satan into a gallop and rode ahead. He dismounted and looked all around, he couldn't see anyone. He knelt down and checked the body. The man was still alive. He was shot through the shoulder and had a grazing head wound. The head wound had bled quite a bit. The shooter must have thought he had killed him.

Orin cleaned the wounds and bandaged him with his spare shirt. The man woke up and immediately grabbed his head. Orin restrained him from pulling off his bandage. The man started to curse Orin and he shouted above him that he hadn't shot him, he just found him on the trail.

The man sat up. He looked all around.

"Where are they?" he asked.

Orin said, "Who?"

"My wife and two daughters and my wagon full of supplies for my trading post."

"I didn't see anyone when I rode up," Orin said.

The man said, "Three men stopped our wagon. They shot me out of my saddle I don't remember anything after that."

Orin stood up. He saw the wagon tracks. They were heading north. He stood on a small rise and scanned the trail. He could see dust rising in the distance. They hadn't traveled too far.

The man tried to stand up and fell down again.

Orin told him, "You're too weak from all of the blood you've lost.

 Where were you traveling to?"

The man explained that they were about a day's ride east of Mesa.

"We have a small community there."

Orin said, "I'm going to put you on my horse. I want you to ride to your town and get medical help. I can track these men on foot. They are going to be slowed down by the wagon. I'll catch them and bring your family back to you. You will just slow me down if you come with me."

Orin put the man on Ole Satan. He tied him on the horse so he wouldn't fall off, started him down the trail and then he turned back. It was time to begin preparing for his mission. He began by taking off his boots and long pants. Nearby, there was a place behind a big rock to cache his things. Removing his shirt and folding his clothes, he placed the items behind the rock, out of sight. Then from the saddlebags he removed a pair of leggings and moccasins and put them on, along with a vest and headband. He placed his bow over his head and across his chest, hung his quiver over the bow and put his gun belt over his shoulder. He was ready.

He looked like an Apache warrior on the war path. In reality he was just that. Finally he placed his rifle on top of his clothes, covered them with brush, and started off on a slow trot. He gathered speed gradually and settled down to a steady comfortable hunter's gait. He smiled to himself. He had missed this since he left his uncle Red Fox.

Orin climbed a small hill and scanned the horizon. The wagon and three horsemen were in sight. They were heading for a stand of trees ahead. Orin thought they were probably going to bed down where the trees were. Veering off the trail, he started running faster. His thought was to go around the trees and come in from behind. Once he reached the tree line from the north, he stopped suddenly. Someone was talking.

Quietly, he glided into the trees. He went ahead cautiously and came to a clearing. He gathered the whole scene at once. There was a water hole among the trees. An old Indian and his squaw were lying on the ground away from the water hole. A young Indian girl was lying nervously in the water near the water's edge. A man was standing over her with her torn dress in his hand. He was taking off his gun belt with the other hand. He warned the two old Indians not to interfere. He turned back to the girl and laughed.

Orin couldn't use his handgun, because that would warn the other men. He readied his bow and took two arrows from the quiver. The first arrow took the man in the shoulder. The force of it turned him so he was facing Orin. The second arrow took him in the throat. Orin dropped his bow and ran forward to catch the man. He dragged him out of the water hole. He took the man's blanket from his saddle and put it around the young Indian girl. She was crying softly. He carried her over to the two old Indians. They were smiling.

Orin said "I'm sorry grandfather that this man has harmed you and your family. I am ashamed that he is of my race."

The old Indian saw the amulet around Orin's neck and exclaimed, "You are a white man but you are also one of us. How can that be?"

Orin said, "I will explain later grandfather, now I must be on my way. Stay here and I will have another horse for you."

He quickly tied the dead man over the saddle on his horse and led him through the trees. He smelled smoke. They had started a campfire. He came closer until he could see the fire. He tied the horse to a sapling and crept forward adjusting his gun belt and tying down his holster. He was ready. The man he had killed must have ridden ahead for water for the camp. Now he only had two men to face.

One of the men approached the wagon.

He said, "I'm not going to tell you again ladies. Throw out your clothes or I'll come in and undress you myself, that's a fact."

Orin could hear the woman and two girls crying. They threw their dresses out of the back of the wagon. The two outlaws started to laugh. Stepping out from the trees Orin told the two men to raise their hands above their heads.

The leader said, "Well looky here we got ourselves a white Indian gunfighter. There are two of us and my brother is in the trees behind you."

Orin said, "You're right, he's behind me all right but he's strapped across his saddle, dead."

When he said that, the two men drew on him. They drew but not fast enough. Orin drew and shot the big man and then the other as his gun cleared his holster. The second man got off a shot into the ground and then fell dead.

Orin gathered up the women's clothes and threw them back into the wagon.

"You can get dressed now ladies," he said.

The women dressed and climbed out of the wagon. They came over to the fire where Orin was sitting. He stood up. They thanked him for coming to their aid.

The women said, "These men killed my husband, I would like to retrieve his body for a proper funeral."

Orin smiled and said, "Your husband isn't dead ma'am. I found him on the trail a while back and treated his wounds. I tied him to my horse and told him to ride home for medical help. I told him I would help you if I could."

The woman and her daughters were smiling as they came up and hugged him.

He said, "I have a few things to do and then we'll be on our way."

He told them about the Indians near the water hole and brought the Indians back with him to the camp.

The women fussed over the young girl and the Indian squaw. They went to the wagon and brought back presents for them. Orin gave two of the horses from the dead men to the Indians. He wrote out a bill of sale for them.

The old Indian was grateful. "What can we do for you my grandson?"

"I will need a travois to carry the bodies of these men back to the authorities. If you could help me build one that would be a great gift from you."

In a very short time, with everyone working together the travois was built. It was strong enough for all three bodies. They wrapped them in their blankets and tied them to the travois. The Indians left camp. They were all riding their own horse now. The Indian girl and squaw were looking at themselves in the hand mirrors that were given to them as gifts. They were happy.

The woman asked Orin what his name was. He had been thinking about this for a while on the trail and decided he had better change his name. They might still be looking for him.

He answered the woman, "My name is John Stanton, from Texas, ma'am."

The woman shook his hand and said, "We are very pleased to meet you, John Stanton. My name is Nora Eddy. These are my daughters Marcie and Gracie."

The girls both curtsied and held out their hands.

He shook them both and then said, "We'd best be getting on ladies. We only have a few hours of daylight left and I have to retrieve my gear back on the trail."

He decided to ride ahead to find his gear before it got dark. Retrieving his items he found everything just as he had left them. The women were almost to the trail when he rode back to join them. They decided it wouldn't be a good idea to travel in the dark, so they set up camp near their original trail.

Everyone was sitting around the fire when Nora said, "John, I think I'd better give you a haircut before we reach our destination. You look more Indian than white and there might be people there who would shoot first and ask questions later."

He reluctantly agreed. The girls were smiling when his long beautiful hair was sheared off. Before long everyone bedded down to rest for the following day's journey.

They arrived at their destination late the next day. They were greeted by Nora's very happy husband, Will. They went through all of the introductions again. Orin officially became John Stanton.

At the trading post John Stanton was treated royally as the guest of honor. Will explained about the trading post to John Stanton, "I originally started it to trade with the Mexicans and Indians, but lately I have a new purpose. This post is now a stopover for the railroad people. They bring wagons and materials and laborers to clear the land for laying tracks here in Arizona. We feed them and give them a good night sleep and they are on the way in the morning. It pays well and we get to meet a lot of new people."

Will went on, "We have had some trouble from the Mexicans lately. The railroad sent some wagons loaded with Chinese laborers and some of them never reached base camp. The Mexicans think the Chinese are cheating them out of their work because they get paid fifty cents a day less than the Mexicans. We have a few hard cases out there in the Mexican community who won't let the Chinese work here in Arizona."

John Stanton asked, "What are the Mexicans doing?"

"They run them off or shoot them. We really don't have the law here like they do in Texas. We are expecting a wagon load of Chinese tomorrow. I hope we don't have any trouble. We have a nice community here and if we have more problems I know some of the people will leave."

John said, "I'm not ready to leave yet maybe I can help."

Nora spoke up, "Let him help Will. I don't think you have ever seen a faster draw or straight shooter than John Stanton."

Will said, "We appreciate any help you can give us."

They unloaded the bodies of the three men and placed them on boards leaning against a hitching post in the back of the building. No one in the community recognized them.

Nora and Will put on a barbecue and after plenty of good conversation they called it a night. John Stanton slept in the barn.

Nora woke up next morning. Marcie was shaking her, "What's wrong Marcie?" she asked.

Marcie looked frightened. She said, "Some Mexicans just rode up and they are telling everyone to leave."

Nora woke Will and told him, "We have a problem I'm going out back to get John."

Marcie said, "I'll do it mama I'm already dressed."

Marcie ran out the back door to get John. Nora dressed and waited for John. He came in shortly he was adjusting his gun belt.

"What's the matter ma'am?" he asked.

"I just looked out the window and saw Hector and Paco Perez. They are two of the leaders of the so called Mexican liberation army. They look like they're up to no good."

Nora and John stepped out on the porch. Paco Perez stared at Nora Eddy with surprise, "Wha…what are you doing here. We heard you were all killed. We came to help out your community."

He stared at the young man standing next to Nora. He noticed the Colt .44 and the way it was tied down.

"Who is this?" he asked.

John answered, "I work for Nora and Will. I'm sort of a handy man." "Where is your husband?" Paco asked.

Nora answered, "He's inside recuperating from two gunshot wounds."

Paco said, "You mean he was shot and still managed to kill three gringos? You married quite a man Mrs. Eddy."

Before Nora could answer, John Stanton cut in, "Mr. Perez, maybe you could identify the men, they are out back."

They walked around to the back of the house. John could see the glint of recognition in Hector's eyes as he viewed the men strapped to the boards.

Paco said, "We do not know these men."

John said, "That's not true. You already knew that there were three of them before you saw them. You must have hired them."

"Boy," Paco said, "you are trying my patience, have you not heard of me and my brother?"

"Just that you two are troublemakers and work for a man named Montoya."

"That is General Montoya and my brother and I are loyal captains in his army of liberation."

John said, "You call it liberating people when you run them out of the territory or kill them?"

"We are liberating the Mexican workers and protecting their jobs," Paco said. He went on, "We know there is a shipment of Chinese workers coming in today. We are here to see that they don't continue on. I have a small army in the hills south of this place. If you help the

Chinese and railroad people we will kill everyone and burn the trading post."

John took a few steps and placed himself directly in front of the Perez brothers.

He said, "I'm here to protect the Eddys' and their post. I have heard of you two. You are thieves and killers who have no regard for people or their property or their lives."

Paco and Hector drew at the same time. They were smiling. John drew and fired twice. They were dead on their feet. The smiles slowly left their faces as they fell to the ground. John sensed someone behind him and turned and fired at one of the Mexicans with a machete in his hands. He heard the boom of a shot gun as Will killed another man ready to strike John Stanton. It was over, the other Mexicans rode off.

They strapped the Perez brothers to a board and put them alongside the other bandits. John told the Eddys about Paco's boast of an army back in the hills. They rounded up all of the horses and put them in the barn. They locked the barn from the inside. John stationed two men in the barn with rifles. He came out of the hayloft on a rope.

"At least they won't be able to steal our horses."

They herded everyone else into the trading post. The men were placed at their posts with a rifle. The women were to be the gun loaders. All sat down to wait. Two hours later, four men rode in. They hailed the trading post.

"Nora and Will Eddy are you in there?" The voice asked.

"It's Cody Mason. I've been appointed marshal of this part of the territory. Are you in there?"

Will cautiously stepped up on the porch. The door was flung open and Nora grabbed Cody and hugged him. Will and John stepped out next and Will made the introductions.

Cody said, "Stanton, eh? Any relation to the Stanton's who have a big ranch near Abilene?"

John said, "No, I'm from the poor Stanton's we are originally from Texas though."

Will and Nora told Cody how John had come to their rescue. Cody thanked John and told him how Will and Nora had helped him ten years ago when he first came to Arizona.

"They are like family to me and I do appreciate what you did for them." He went on, "Let's check on the hooligans you got out back. Cody whistled loudly when he saw the five bodies.

He turned to John and said, "I hope you have deep pockets."

John said, "What do you mean by that?"

Cody answered, "There is a bounty on all of those men. You have about two thousand seven hundred dollars coming to you. The railroad pays good to eliminate the bad guys. They have interfered with railroad business and their workers and customers for too long, you just did them a big favor."

John couldn't believe it. He could even start his own ranch someday soon. He smiled. They all turned to the south; there was the sound of shooting coming from the hills.

Cody said, "Don't worry folks; we heard that the Mexicans were planning something for today so we set a trap for them. I sent twenty men on either side of the pass. It sounds like they have a little war going on. I'm going to join them."

He looked at John, "Want to ride along?"

"I sure do," he said.

They rode up to Cody's men an hour later. The battle was over the Mexican's were routed. They had captured one of the Mexicans. He told them that General Montoya was on his way with his army. The Chinese and all those who were helping them would be killed and the trading post burned to the ground. Cody sent a rider back to Fort Defiance for help.

Cody explained to John about Juan Montoya.

"He put on a light blue uniform top and called himself a general. He has been chased out of Mexico because he is a sadistic killer and bandit. He wants to establish an empire for himself in Arizona territory. The Mexicans love him. They think he is their savior." He went on, "We have tried to stop him in the past but he is a brilliant strategist. He always has some kind of escape plan."

John said, "Cody, if Montoya is coming the same way as those other Mexicans, I think we can get him this time."

"What do you mean, John?"

"I checked the route that the Mexicans used to run away from your men. I used my telescope. They had to go through a narrow gorge. The hills close in about forty or fifty feet in the opening. We will wait until we know that we can get Montoya."

Cody said, "It sounds good let's go back to the post and work on it. I'll leave some lookouts to warn us when he comes."

When they reached the trading post John asked Will if he had any good rifles in stock.

Will said, "I have some I took in trade about five years ago but I haven't been able to sell or trade them. Look them over and take what you need."

John found what he was looking for right away; an old sharps buffalo gun. "Do you have ammunition for this one?"

He answered, "I have plenty of ammunition for all of the rifles. Are you sure you want that one? It's kind of hard to handle."

John said, "My father taught me how to shoot a rifle and he had a buffalo gun just like this one. I'll only need one shot from it and then I'll use the Winchester."

Cody said, "You're pretty sure of yourself, John."

"Yes, I am. I had a good teacher. I would like to sight it in first."

John took the buffalo gun and a box of shells out back to practice to sight it in.

An hour later he came back and said, "I'm ready."

Cody said, "You have to get him with the first shot John, if you don't he'll be long gone."

"Set up a target for me. Put it out at least five hundred yards."

Cody set up the target and stood out of the way of it. John readied the rifle and took his shot. Cody brought the target back to the onlookers.

He walked up to John and said, "Mr. I hope we never have a quarrel between us. I would hate to have you as an enemy."

He unfolded the target; it was the size of a man. If it had been a man the left side of his chest would have been blown away. Cody, John, and four other riflemen went back to the gorge to make their plans. They found three good spots to shoot from and decided to use all of them. They piled up brush to conceal themselves.

They went into the gorge and looked back at their positions to see what the Mexicans would see when they came out at the end of the gorge. Everything looked normal.

One of the men said, "Cody a rider's coming in behind us."

They all rode out quickly and hid behind some boulders. It was one of Cody's lookouts. Cody rode out to meet him.

"Cody, they are about a half a day behind me. I didn't stop to count them...looks like a hundred or more."

Cody said, "Let's get our gear set up gentlemen."

They rode back to the trading post and warned everyone that Montoya was coming. The men filled their canteens and Nora passed out food that the women had prepared for them.

Once they packed everything they rode back to their ambush spot and settled in to wait. They could see the dust rising when the Mexicans entered the gorge. John jammed a forked stick in the ground and laid his rifle barrel in the fork. He told Cody that it would really steady his barrel for his one-time shot.

Cody said, "Remember John, Montoya will be wearing a light blue jacket."

"Just make sure Cody. Use my telescope to make sure that it's him."

Cody nodded and took up the scope. They were coming closer. Cody squinted through the telescope. He picked out the blue jacket right away. He brought the telescope up to the face of the rider.

"What the hell, it's not him," he murmured. He checked the riders on either side of the blue jacket.

"There you are," he said.

"John can you see the blue jacket yet?"

John answered, "Yes."

"Count two men over from the blue jacket. He's wearing a black vest with red trim on it. Do you see him?"

"Yes," John answered. He has a black hat with red trim on it too." "That's him," Cody said. Take your shot whenever you're ready."

All of the men readied their rifles. John's shot was the signal to open fire. John took careful aim. This was a moving target. He had to lead him just right. There wasn't much of a wind so the bullet should go true. He took a long breath and then exhaled slowly. When his breath was gone he squeezed the trigger gently. The old buffalo boomed. The riflemen sprayed a deadly fire on the approaching Mexicans.

Montoya was blown off his horse. His men tried to reach for him but they came under a deadly hail of gunfire. They were bunched up in front, they couldn't advance or retreat. They were cut down as they milled around at the head of the gorge. The men in the rear finally got turned around and headed out the way they had come in. The rifle fire followed them. More Mexicans fell. It was a slaughter. The ones who got away wouldn't be coming back. Cody and John rode down to find Montoya. He looked peaceful in death.

Cody said, "I don't believe it. It was too easy. I never thought we would ever get this devil. You did good John, thank you."

They gathered up all of the weapons, horses, and Montoya's body and headed back to the trading post. Cody and John were riding side by side.

Cody looked at John and said, "You'd better get deeper pockets. This guy has at least a two thousand dollar bounty on him."

John said, "You should share with me on this one. If I had shot the man in the blue jacket Montoya might have gotten away."

Cody tried to protest but John wouldn't hear of it. They shook hands and rode to the trading post.

Two days later John and Cody headed for Fort Defiance. John would collect the rest of his reward for Montoya. The rewards would total four thousand seven hundred dollars altogether. Enough to buy a small spread somewhere. When they arrived at Fort Defiance, they reported to the commanding officer, Angus MacDonald. He pored over all of the affidavits pertaining to Montoya's death. He was satisfied.

He asked, "How would you like to be paid?"

When John explained that he and Cody would split the reward, Cody resisted.

"No sir," he said, "John deserves it all. I want none of it."

John told Colonel MacDonald that the railroad gave him a bank draft that could be drawn on any bank in the States or its territories.

He went on "I would accept a bank draft from you also, Colonel. It would be easier to travel with. I would like one hundred in cash if that's permissible."

The Colonel agreed and sent his aide to prepare the bank draft and the cash.

"You have done a great service for your country in eliminating that renegade scourge, the Colonel said, "Arizona territory will be a lot safer for its people to live now."

Later, outside the Colonel's office, Cody said, "Well John I know you want to head up to Montana so I'll leave you now. I have been appointed Chief Federal Marshall for the territories so I have to get back to work."

They shook hands and left. Cody headed south and John headed east back through New Mexico. John spent two weeks traveling through to Santa Fe up through to Raton, up north.

John headed north into Colorado territory. He was fixing some fish over a small fire, it was dusk and he had been traveling for two days. He was being watched by someone.

When the fish were cooked he spoke up in a loud voice. He spoke in Apache.

"If you two are hungry come to my fire and share my food. If you don't show yourselves, I will treat you as my enemy."

A voice was heard in the darkness, "Hold brother, we thought you were a white man. We are coming out now."

John Stanton turned around as they stood behind him. The young Indian exclaimed, "You are a white man."

He reached for his knife but the other older Indian put his hand on his arm.

"Look brother, at the amulet he is wearing. He is the one, Red Fox's nephew. They came forward and clapped their arms on his shoulder.

"You are one of us." They were both smiling.

When they had their fill of fish they sat around the fire talking. One of the Indians said, "We have heard of your troubles in Texas. How might we help you?"

John said, "I'm on a pilgrimage to Montana. I told my father that I would follow his footsteps to the beautiful territory of Montana before I choose a place to live."

The older Indian said "It is a wise man who listens to his father in these matters. I will show you the quickest and safest way to travel through Colorado. I can only give you an idea how to travel through Wyoming territory. The most important thing to remember is this: Winter is not far behind us. In northern Colorado, northern Wyoming and Montana the cold, and the wind, and snow can and will kill you. You must prepare for it. We will start of tomorrow early."

Two days later they saw the tracks of three riders traveling ahead of them. They were fresh tracks and not too far ahead of them. The Indians suggested resting in a small grove of trees. John Stanton rode ahead to check out the three riders.

He found them laying an ambush for someone about three miles down the road. He reached for his telescope and checked out the horizon ahead. He spied a wagon with two men on the front seat and one man in back with the cargo they were carrying. It was too late to go back to the camp for help. He had to do this on his own. He tried to signal the oncoming wagon but the sun was not cooperating. It was too cloudy. He tied off his horse, checked his rifle and handgun, and then proceeded to get closer.

The ambushers got the drop on the three men in the wagon.

The leader shouted, "Drop your guns on the ground or we'll shoot you dead!"

The men complied and were ordered out off the wagon. One of the ambushers checked the contents of the wagon and said, "Manny, we really done good this time. I see gold and silver."

The leader said, "I told you not to use our names now we have to kill them all."

One of the men from the wagon said, "The young man in our party is the mine owner's son. If you kill him his father will run you into your grave."

Manny said, "That may be true if they found you three but there's a hole in the ground beneath the big rock behind us that seems to go on forever. We'll just drop you in the hole and roll another rock over it. They'll never find you. His pappy will think you three ran off with his money."

The ambushers herded the three men behind the rock. John had no other choice. He couldn't just confront them, he had to shoot them. He leveled his rifle on the leader and fired. He quickly swung over to the next man and fired again. By the time the third man turned in his direction, he fired a third time.

The three men from the wagon slowly turned around.

"Are you alright?" John asked.

"Yes sir," the young man said, "You saved us in the nick of time."

The older man asked, "Who are you, sir?"

"My name is John Stanton from Abilene Texas. I spotted these men setting an ambush and I waited to see what they were up to."

The young man seemed nervous.

"Mr. Stanton let us get our guns. Two Indians are coming up behind you."

John laughed, "They are with me. I'm on my way to Montana and they are guiding me."

The men relaxed.

John said, "Let's not let that hole go to waste. Strip those dirty ambushers and do what they were going to do to you."

Later, they were going through the ambushers things when the young man said, "I found a wanted poster on one of them. They really are bad men. Mr. Stanton, if you come with us I'm sure my father will see that you get the reward for them and for saving our cargo."

"I'd like to oblige but winter is coming fast and we have to get back on the trail again. We will take their horses and guns with us. You can collect the reward."

They all shook hands and went their separate ways. They traveled faster now and were soon in Wyoming territory. They all marveled at the scenery in Colorado and now were enjoying Wyoming just as much.

The older Indian spoke to John, "I have not gone farther than this in Wyoming territory but if you just keep traveling north you should reach your destination. My nephew and I must leave you now."

They clapped their hands on their shoulders as a sign of respect.

John said, "Wait a moment. I want to give you a paper saying you bought these horses from me. I am still a lawman from Arizona. My name will give you safe passage for you and you nephew. Take the rifles too; they will just weigh me down."

They thanked him and left smiling.

CHAPTER TEN

John woke up suddenly. Something was wrong. The fire had gone out and it was snowing heavily. He had best be on his way. He saddled Ole Satan and put his gear on the pack horse and headed north. He didn't realize that he was already in Montana territory. All of the passes were filling with snow. He urged the horses onward. He had to find a cabin or a town of some kind soon. He was chilled to the bone. The pack horse was stumbling along. He stopped long enough to transfer his saddlebags to Ole Satan.

The snow let up some and he could see that he was on a large mesa. He came near the edge and looked down. He thought he saw a light flickering in the distance. He urged his mount back and forth trying to find a path down into the valley below. He found a spot that he could navigate and started down.

He held the reins of his pack horse as they moved slowly along. The pack horse slipped, panicked and then bolted past John and Ole Satan before it fell over the side of the trail into mid-air. John let go of the reins and watched the pack horse as he fell down the mountain.

John made it to the floor of the valley but he couldn't see anything. The snow came down harder. He wanted to stop and build a fire but he knew if he stopped now, he was a dead man. He coaxed Ole Satan onward. He was freezing. He was starting to lose consciousness. All of a sudden he started to feel warm again and then the darkness clouded his mind.

MONTANA TERRITORY

Moses Dern was trying to stay on track with the sleigh he was driving. His boss Maggie Enders and her daughter Elizabeth were riding in back under a few blankets. They were on the way back to their ranch after a day of celebrating the birth of a new Montana cowboy at their neighbors. The two women huddled together, closer, for warmth.

Elizabeth raised the blanket for a gulp of fresh air. She saw something at the side of the trail near a big pine tree.

She hollered out, "Moses, stop, please." Moses dutifully stopped the sleigh.

"What is it, miss?"

"I saw a man on a horse they were leaning against a tree."

Moses got out of the sleigh and backtracked about fifty feet. Sure enough there was a horse and rider. He waded into the deep snow and stopped at the tree.

"Can I help you sir?"

No answer. The man's chin lay on his chest. His eyes looked like they were frozen shut. Ice was forming on his beard. His clothes were wet and frozen to his saddle. Moses took the horses reins and urged him on to the trail behind the sleigh. He tied the reins to the back of the sleigh.

Moses got back into the driver's seat. He said, "Ladies we have to get to the ranch as soon as possible. I don't know if he's alive or dead. He is frozen to his saddle and his horse is not in good shape either."

The women urged him to hurry home.

Ole Satan sensed that they were helping them and tried to trot along as best he could.

They reached the ranch house and went right to the barn.

Maggie said, "Moses, try to cut him away from the saddle, we'll go to the house and get things ready for him."

The women went into the house. Elizabeth stirred up the fire and went for more firewood. Maggie got blankets and pillows and an old night shirt that had belonged to her husband who was now deceased. Maggie made a bed in front of the fireplace.

Moses came running in to the ranch house. "I need help ladies I can't carry him alone."

They rushed back to the barn. The man's pants were practically cut off. Moses wrapped a horse blanket around him and they half carried and half dragged him to his place at the fireplace. After he got him settled, Moses went back to the barn to tend to the horse.

The women stripped off the man's wet clothes. Elizabeth was visibly shaken. She had never seen a naked man before.

Maggie smiled and said, "Come on Lizzie, help me put your pa's night shirt on him. Let's dry him really good, his skin is like ice."

Lizzie blushed and turned her head. Maggie said, "Lizzie this is a man, if I was forty years younger I'd give you a run for him."

They both smiled. They piled blankets on the man.

"Lizzie," Maggie said, "Go put on your night gown this man is going to need our body heat. The blankets aren't enough."

When Lizzie returned her mother was already in her night gown and under the covers. The man was lying on his left side and Maggie was right up against his back.

Lizzie crawled under the covers and shivered from the cold coming from the man's body.

"Come on girl push up against him, he needs your warmth."

Lizzie did as she was told. They all started to warm up and the man even moaned a bit, then fell asleep.

Maggie woke up to her daughters screams. "What's the matter honey?" she asked.

"Mama, he peed on me! I'm soaking wet!" She shuddered when she said that.

Maggie said, "Well at least we know that part of him is working again. That's a good sign."

"But mama he peed on me."

"Well Lizzie, look at it this way, it could have been worse, what if the other side started working, where would that leave me?"

"Oh, mama," Lizzie grieved.

Then both women started laughing hysterically.

"Bring me another night shirt then go clean up", Maggie said.

Maggie bathed the man and put the other night shirt on him. Boy she thought aloud, "You are quite a specimen. I hope you and Lizzie hit it off in the future."

The man moaned and then was quiet again. Moses came in for breakfast in the morning.

"I've never seen finer horseflesh in my life. It has a strong heart and is recovering nicely."

Moses lived in the barn and had his own fireplace. The warmth of the fire put new life into Ole Satan. He had a new blanket and was being fed well.

Moses asked, "Has he woke up yet?"

"No but he is thawing out well," replied Maggie as she prepared some soup waiting for the man to wake up.

Moses spoke up, "I had a hard time getting his side arm off. The way it was tied down. I figure he must really know how to use it. He could come in pretty handy around here. I didn't go into his saddlebags because that isn't my way."

"Thank you for all of your help Moses."

Moses went back to the barn to tend to the man's horse. He rubbed him down again, replaced his blanket, and fed and watered him again.

The man had another accident the next night but the women had him padded like a newborn; neither one was touched.

They laughed again at Maggie's earlier remarks.

John woke up on the third day. He saw a woman sitting in a rocking chair.

"Where am I?"

"You are in the great territory of Montana. You are resting on the Enders's ranch of which I am the owner."

He tried to sit up and fell back.

"Take it easy mister, you aren't ready to go back to work yet."

She sat him up and propped a few pillows behind him. "I'll get you some homemade soup and bread. You need plenty of nourishment but you have to take it easy. Don't rush things."

"You saved my life, how am I going to thank you?"

"Oh, I've got a few ways. You can help me run the ranch once you're better. I can't get help from town. The bank wants to foreclose but they have to wait until spring to do it. The townspeople have been warned to stay away from the ranch."

John had rested over the past two weeks and was now fully recovered. He and Ole Satan rode out to the ranch's boundaries and checked out the cattle that had wintered in a partially protected valley. He came back to the ranch.

"Mrs. Enders, you are going to need some more ranch hands to run this ranch."

"I know", Maggie said. If I had a few more hands I could round up enough cattle to make my payroll and payment to the bank."

"As I said," she continued, "The townspeople have been warned not to help me. They are all afraid."

John asked, "Is there another town nearby that I could possibly hire a few men?"

"There is a community about twenty five miles west of here."

"I don't know if any men are available there and please stop calling me Mrs. Enders my name is Maggie. And another thing you are my new foreman, we'll work out the details later."

"Thank you Maggie", he said, "We are going to make this a working ranch again. Have Moses clean out the bunkhouse, I'm going to get a crew to help us."

John saddled up Ole Satan and rode west. It was closer to thirty miles but he found the community he was looking for. Like all the towns and communities he had visited there was a saloon.

The community was a poor one. None of the men were playing cards. They were just nursing their beer and acting like nothing bothered them. John walked up to a table and asked if anyone needed or wanted to work.

One of the men said, "Who's asking?"

John answered, "I'm the foreman of the Enders's ranch about thirty miles due east of here. My boss asked me to hire on a few hands to help round up the cattle. It might work into a full time job. Anyone interested?"

One of the older men stood up and said, "A man came by a few months ago and told us we would be welcome anywhere in their community except working on the Enders's ranch. It wasn't a statement it was a warning. The man looked and acted like a gunfighter. We took the hint and didn't go in that direction. Now why would he do that mister?"

John said, "The Enders's ranch is run by a widow named Maggie Enders. Her husband was shot and killed a few years ago and she has done her very best trying to run the ranch herself. Some of her hands left because they didn't like taking orders from a woman others were driven off. Her cattle is scattered all over the range. We need people to gather a herd for sale. She will pay the going rate for cow hands but can't pay until the cattle are sold."

The older man stepped forward, "I've been around cattle all of my life. I would be proud to work for the Enders's ranch."

Four more men stood up and said the same. The last man stood up and said, "I don't like people who treat women poorly, I'm also handy with a gun and I'd be proud to join you."

John smiled and said, "Bartender give these men another drink on me."

He turned to the men at the table and said, "We leave in an hour get your gear and meet me out front."

The next day when they reached the Enders's ranch John made all of the introductions and when the men went into the bunk house he turned to Maggie and said, "I think we have gotten a good crew."

The older man they hired was named Carl Johnson. He was worth his weight in gold. He had indeed worked around cattle all his life. He worked as hard as anyone to bring the cattle to the ranch holding area.

John and Carl rode into the nearest town to see if any cattle buyers were around. They found one at the hotel dining room. His name was Myles Anderson. He was also a ranking member of the cattleman's association. He was more interested in buying in the spring but he said he could use some now if they had wintered well. They rode out to the ranch.

After the introductions to Maggie and Lizzie they took Myles out to the corral holding about one hundred head of cattle that they had rounded up. Myles Anderson was impressed with what he saw.

He said, "If all of your cattle are in this condition I'll buy the whole herd this spring."

John said, "That's fine Mr. Anderson but Mrs. Enders is in need of some cash now to make up her mortgage payment."

One of the hands rode up. He hollered out. "Mrs. Enders needs you Mr. Stanton."

They all rode back to the ranch house. There were three men talking to Maggie Enders. She was crying and Lizzie was trying to console her.

John asked, "What's going on here?"

Maggie said, "John, they're taking my ranch from me."

John turned to the three men, "I'm John Stanton, the foreman here, what's the problem, gentlemen?"

One man spoke up, "I'm Emmet Blair. I represent the County Bank. This gentleman is the sheriff from town and the other gentleman is George Ernst. He handles all of the bank's legal affairs." He went on, "Mrs. Enders is in arrears on her mortgage payments and we are formally announcing procedures to foreclose on this property."

He had a smug look on his face as the other two men nodded in agreement to what he had just said.

John said, "Mrs. Enders has until next week to make up the payments. We are considering selling the herd to this gentleman in the spring. Could we have a little more time?"

Emmet Blair laughed and said, "That's out of the question. We have a bank to run and rules to follow."

John asked, "How much is Mrs. Enders in arrears?"

Emmet Blair pored over some papers that George Ernst handed him and said, "It looks like she will have to pay off the total amount. It comes to just about three thousand and seven hundred dollars."

John said, "Wait a moment."

He went into the ranch and returned with all of the bank drafts that he had. He signed them over to Maggie Enders and handed them to Ernst Blair.

Blair said, "What is this?"

John explained what they were and then said, "These will more than cover the payments, make sure Maggie is credited with the amount left over. I'll be in town tomorrow to check her account."

Blair sputtered, "You, --You can't do this, we have started foreclosure proceedings."

John said, "Ask your lawyer friend. If Maggie makes the payment before next week your procedure doesn't mean a thing."

The lawyer nodded in agreement.

John went on, "We have a darn good witness to the payment in Mr. Anderson here. He is with the cattleman's association."

Blair took the bank drafts and rode off. The other two followed him.

Anderson said, "John it looks like you made an enemy of Mr. Blair. He was going to steal this ranch and you stopped him."

Maggie threw her arms around John and cried. When she settled down, she said, "I'll pay you back as soon as possible."

John said, "Don't worry about it. You saved my life, this is the least I could do."

Myles Anderson said, "I can give you a check to tide you over until spring if you like."

Maggie agreed to take a thousand dollar check to guarantee the sale of the herd to Myles Anderson's group.

Later John was sitting on the front porch and Elizabeth Enders walked up to him and put her hands to his face and gave him a gentle kiss.

She then said, "You saved our ranch John how can we ever repay you?"

John said, "Well that was a darn good down payment you just made. Let's work out the details. I will need one of those payments a couple of times a day."

Lizzie laughed. "You drive a hard bargain but I'll do my best to oblige."

They both laughed and knew that this was the start of something that they had known was coming.

Three months later they were joined in wedlock at the Enders's ranch.

John Stanton, AKA, Orin Sanger embarked on a new era. It wasn't long before Lizzie informed him that he was to become a father. He celebrated long and hard with the ranch hands.

Spring was just around the corner. The snow was going fast. The cattle roundup would soon begin. There was a lot of excitement in the air.

One of the hands hollered out, "Rider coming in!"

John watched the approaching rider. He rode that horse like someone that he knew.

"By golly," he thought, *'it is him'*. "Cody Mason what are you doing in Montana?!"

Cody dismounted and approached John. He said, "I'm here on business and I have some bad news for you, John."

"What is it Cody?"

Cody answered, "The Eddy's were massacred. Will was shot and the mother and daughters were brutally raped and shot. The trading post was burned to the ground and everyone that wasn't killed was run off. From what I found out it was the work of renegade white men that the Mexicans had hired to avenge their losses."

"One woman and her small daughter escaped by hiding in an old root cellar. She said the gang was run by two men with strange hats. One man wore a top hat and the other younger one wore one of the English bowler hats. They raped the women first and then turned them over to the rest of the gang. She heard them screaming and finally heard the shots that put them out of their misery."

John asked, "Did you find them?"

Cody answered, "I've been tracking them for about two months.

They split up in Colorado but from the description of the two hats that the men wore, the two leaders are here in Montana somewhere. They are also known to be rustlers."

Lizzie and Maggie came out to the porch and John informed them as to what had happened. He told them that he had to help Cody find them.

As he was about to get his gear one of the hands rode up. His horse was all lathered up from the fast ride.

He said, "We have got some trouble Mr. Stanton. Two of our hands were gunned down and quite a bit of cattle have been run off."

Carl Johnson spoke up, "You stay here John, I can take the rest of the hands and track them down. I have a lot of experience in these matters."

John said, "No Carl, I want you to take over as foreman of the ranch. You watch over the women I'll do the tracking, I was taught by the very best."

Carl laughed, "The best tracker in the western territory is Red Fox, an Apache."

"I know," John said, "he is my adopted Uncle. I'll tell you all about it someday. I'm very good at what I do."

He turned to Cody and said, "Want to ride along Cody? We might run into the men you're looking for."

Cody said, "I'd be glad to give you a hand. Would you send someone back to town for the two marshals that were riding with me? We could use a couple of more guns on our side."

John told one of the men to do that and then they all mounted up and started after the rustlers. They rode to where the cattle had wintered and buried the two ranch hands that had been shot. They had been dead for about a week.

The cattle left a broad trail for the first few days but then the tracks were harder to see because of the cattle drives that had started. They also ran into rocks and sand. John thought to himself, "This isn't even a good test for the Indian trackers that he had trained." The rustlers were in for a rude awakening.

John went on ahead on the fourth day while the rest of the men made camp. He rode in to camp a few hours later.

"I located the herd. They are in a valley on the other side of those hills over there. I also saw where their lookouts were posted. We shouldn't have any trouble if we leave at dusk."

They all ate and then tended to their weapons. They rode off at dusk and arrived a few hours later.

John said, "I'll go in first. When I want you to come in their camp I'll give you a signal like the sound of an old hoot owl."

After he removed his gun belt, boots, and hat, he left his things with the man assigned to watch the horses. He put on his moccasins and a band around his head and jammed his revolver down in his belt around his back.

He found the first outpost in about an hour. The man was dozing. John struck him with a rock and really put him to sleep. He tied his hands and feet and gagged him with his own kerchief. It took him a half hour to dispose of the second outpost.

He spotted the third man in the rustler's camp. He had just put a couple of logs on their community fire. John hooted a few times. The man on guard was alert and suspicious. He stood up and started walking around. He came around the far side of the campfire and leaned against a tree. He stood there listening for a long time. He heard the men coming through the trees, he turned to warn the sleeping men near the fire and found himself staring into the barrel of John's gun.

John said, "Drop your rifle or I'll put a bullet right between your eyes."

The frightened rustler dropped his rifle. John turned to the sleeping men. The first man he saw had a bowler hat over his face. As he turned back to the other lookout the man let out a yell. John struck him on the temple with his revolver and ran over to the man with the bowler hat.

The man started to get up and John covered him with his revolver. He told the man to stand up with his hands in the air. He did as he was told. John fired a shot in the air and then put the gun to the rustler leaders head and said, "Tell your men to lay down their weapons or I'll shoot you first and then we'll get the rest of you."

All of the rustlers were up and reaching for their weapons. When John's voice rang out, "You men raise your hands in the air or my people will shoot you down!"

One of the rustlers said, "What people? All I see is one man, you can't shoot us all."

A voice came out of the darkness. "I'll take him first if he moves toward his gun, John."

The rest of the posse talked it up so that the rustlers could see that they were surrounded. They all stood up and raised their hands. John quickly disarmed them and tied them hand and foot. He caught sight of the man with the top hat. He singled him out and took him along with the man with the bowler hat over to Cody.

"Got a present for you, Cody."

"Cody smiled, "You did a good service here John I'm taking them back to Arizona for a quick trial."

The two men protested. They knew what was waiting for them in Arizona; The hangman's knot.

Cody took the two men back to the Enders's ranch and locked them in a shed. He left them tied up and helpless. John sent three men to escort the prisoners to town to the sheriff's office. The rest of the men started the herd for the journey back to the ranch.

It took three days before the cattle were back where they belonged. John told Cody that he could leave the prisoners with him and they would be tried as rustlers - Another hanging offense.

Cody said, "No, but thanks anyway. Arizona wants these men badly. We have to set an example with them. I just want the two leaders from the Arizona murders. You can have the rest for rustling your cattle and shooting your cowhands."

"Cody, do you mind if I talk to the two men before you leave? I think I can get them to tell me who's behind the rustling."

"Okay, John," he said, "I'd like to get going in about two days."

"Maggie and Lizzie's cooking will more than make up for the wait," John said.

John had the young prisoner with the top hat brought out behind the Enders's barn. Two of the hands had dug a grave by his orders. The young man showed a lot of bravado. When John questioned him he refused to answer or name anyone.

John showed him the grave. He said, "Unless you tell me who hired you, this is your last stop."

The young man protested, "Wait a minute I have to be tried in front of a jury before I get sentenced."

"Not out here, I'm the judge and the jury I will shoot you here and now. You'd better hope you're dead before I bury you. I'm not even going to check."

He cocked the .44 and put it to the man's head.

"I can't talk my partner will kill me."

"I'll fix it so he thinks I killed you he won't even know that I didn't."

"All right take the gun away. I'll talk. The head man is Blair from the bank and that lawyer side-kick of his. The man who recruited us is the sheriff. They have a good thing going for them here. They want to control as much land as they can. They didn't tell me why. We were just supposed to run as many ranchers off their land as we could. That's the truth."

John said, "Good, now climb down into the hole, I'm going to cover your head with a cloth and then sprinkle some dirt on it and your body. I'm going to fire two shots in the air and after a few minutes we'll bring your partner out here to see your grave. Don't move or say anything. Breathe shallow. We'll see how brave he is."

The man with the bowler hat came out guarded by two of John's men.

He said, "You must be trying to scare me into talking, well it ain't gonna work. Where's my little buddy at? I bet he didn't talk neither."

John led him over to the gravesite.

"There he is. You might be joining him in just a minute, there's plenty of room. If you don't tell me who put you up to rustling our cattle I'm going to give you the same sentence that I gave your friend."

He took out his colt and held it to the man's head.

"Before you say anything, here in Montana on the ranch, I'm the only judge and jury that you get."

The man said, "Wait a minute mister, you didn't have to kill my little buddy. We would have told you. The sheriff hired us to lead the gang. His boss is the banker Blair. The lawyer is in on it too."

John called his two ranch hands over and asked them to pull the young man out of the grave. John told the two desperados that the marshal would have strung him up if he had shot either of them. They were locked away in the tool shed again.

John's men returned from town and reported that the sheriff had locked the rustlers up and that John and Mrs. Enders should come in and file charges against them.

John and Cody rode in the next day. The town was in an uproar. The deputy sheriff had been shot and the prisoners and the sheriff were gone. The owner of the bank came up and said his bank had been robbed of all his cash. Mr. Blair was missing. They checked the lawyer's office. He was gone as well.

John said to Cody and the town elders, "They must have known that we would find out about them through the prisoners that we had taken."

Cody said "I'll find a town with a telegraph and notify everyone to watch for them all."

John organized a posse, but it was to no avail. With all of the horsemen and cattle tracks around it would be an impossibility to find their tracks. John and Cody headed back to the Enders ranch. Cody and his men loaded up the two killers and headed for Arizona.

Just before he left, Cody told John "You did well son, he handed him a badge. Use it when you think you might need it. I'll stand up for you whatever happens."

They shook hands and he left.

When John went into the house he had a surprise waiting for him.

Maggie Enders and Carl Johnson were sitting at the table holding hands and giggling like two young children.

Maggie told him, "John, Carl and I took to one another as soon as we met; we've been together as much as we would ever since. We aren't getting any younger. We are going to get married and go to Santa Fe for our honeymoon."

John's face broke into a big smile. "I'm happy for the two of you, Maggie. You couldn't ask for a better man."

Three days later they were married and were off on their honeymoon. They said they'd be back before round up was over.

John and his ranch hands mended fences, put out more feed to fatten the cattle for the roundup, and kept a keen eye out for anymore rustlers.

The snow was almost gone. The rivers were overflowing. Everyone was looking forward to spring, especially Elizabeth Stanton. She could hardly wait to show off her round belly to some of her friends.

John told her that when they were all caught up with their work he would take her in a buggy to visit all of her friends. Lizzie was too excited, she couldn't wait.

Lizzie had Moses hitch up her buggy. He tried to tell her that the trails were not good after all of the snow melt. There had been a lot of flooding. She insisted so he hitched up her buggy and she was on her way to go visiting.

She decided not to take the main road. Instead she took the path that went toward the river. There was an old bridge crossing the river that she had used many times with her father when she was younger.

The swift running water was deep. It came almost to the bottom of the bridge. The pilings were exposed from the hammering of the swift water. The bridge was swaying. Lizzie took no notice of this. She was lost in thought about how happy everyone would be. The horse trotted on to the bridge and started across. Lizzie heard the foundation go from the weight of the buggy. It swayed over and with a loud crash the bridge and horse and buggy fell into the river.

The horse ended upside down and floundered around until he finally succumbed to the river. Lizzie was thrown into the river. She struck her head on part of the bridge and was dazed. The swift moving water dragged her farther downstream.

Her clothing was caught in the roots of a tree hanging over the river. She couldn't break loose, she was completely underwater. The water was as cold as ice and merciless. Her last thoughts were of her poor husband and baby.

John returned to the ranch with the ranch hands. They were exhausted and excited about a job well done. They were ready for the roundup. Moses met John at the door.

"Mr. John, Mrs. Lizzie left two days ago to go visiting and she hasn't returned yet. I'm worried."

John got a couple of volunteers and headed out to the main road. They had only traveled a few miles when one of the men said, "I don't even see any tracks of the buggy here, John."

John wheeled his horse around and said, "Follow me. She probably took the old track across the bridge."

When they arrived at the bridge, John slumped in the saddle, "Lord, please don't let it end like this."

He jumped to the ground and went into the river. He saw the horse and buggy. He went under the buggy, Lizzie was gone.

He hollered out, "Search both sides of the river!"

One of the men spotted Lizzie's foot sticking out of the water. John waded into the river and went under the water to free her. It took a few tries but he finally freed her. John sent one of the men to get some blankets and a wagon. Lizzie's face was white as marble. John gathered her in his arms and placed her in the wagon. He rode in back and held her in his arms until they reached the ranch house.

Bill Nolan, his right hand man, came up to him and said, "John do you want me to send for the undertaker?"

John nodded and said, "Yes, but ask him to come tomorrow morning. I'll have her clothes all laid out for her."

John carried his wife into the bedroom and laid her on the bed. He brushed all the tangles and twigs out of her hair. He went though her clothes and picked out things she really liked. Tears were rolling down his cheeks all the while he fussed over her.

He lay nested to her and held her hand. He sobbed just like he did when his mother had died. He thought, "Why do the people I love the most have to be taken from me?"

He soon fell asleep.

CHAPTER ELEVEN

Bill Nolan woke him in the morning, "John, the undertaker is here."

"Thanks Bill, I'll be right with you."

He pulled the blanket up to Lizzie's neck and left to join the others.

The undertaker asked, "Where would you like to lay your wife to rest, Mr. Stanton?"

John waved him over to the window and said, "Do you see that knoll out there with the pretty little tree on it. She loved to set there with her momma and sew baby clothes. That's where I want her laid to rest."

When the undertaker inquired about a coffin, Bill Nolan cut in the conversation, "Mr. Undertaker, the boys and I will be bringing in the coffin to you tomorrow."

Bill turned to John, "John we started work on it last night. I hope you don't mind. We'd be right proud if you would let us do this."

John said, "I really appreciate it Bill. I know Lizzie is smiling down on you and the boys right now."

The undertaker left the ranch house with Lizzie and an escort of four ranch hands. They had all loved her as a sister.

John went out to the knoll and started digging her grave. Bill joined him and they soon had it done. They cleaned the site of all the debris and started planning where the memorial garden would be.

The local minister came out to see John. They talked for several hours and finally agreed on a small service in about three days. Then when Maggie and Carl returned they would have a big service and a wake with all of Lizzie's friends.

John counted the days until Maggie and Carl returned. When John gave them the news, Maggie fainted dead away.

They carried her to her bed and John told Carl, "Don't leave her for a moment. She is really going to need your support now. Lizzie was her reason for living this long."

Maggie joined the living three days later. She came up to John, "John, I'm so terribly sorry. I acted if I was the only one who had lost a loved one, you must be devastated."

He put his arms around her and they both cried.

After the second gravesite service they held a big wake at the ranch. All of the neighbors and townspeople came. Everyone had a story to tell about Lizzie. They all left later, knowing they had lost a truly loving friend.

Two days later, John asked Maggie and Carl to join him at the table. He said, "I have a story to tell the two of you and when I'm done,

I'm going to be on my way to Abilene, Texas."

He told them of the killings on his father's ranch and everything that had happened to him since then, going from a fugitive to a lawman. He showed them his marshal's badge.

"I'm sorry Maggie and Carl but I have to go home. I haven't seen my father in years. I can't even remember how many."

Maggie protested, "John, a third of this ranch is yours, I'll see that you get your share."

"Don't worry about it folks I'll be leaving now."

He hugged them both and mounted Ole Satan and rode off. Tears were streaming down his cheeks again.

CHAPTER TWELVE

John rode into Abilene about a month later. He took a room at the hotel and slept for about ten hours. He woke up ate at a restaurant and left for the ranch. He was getting excited now. No one had recognized him. He had registered as John Stanton.

As he approached the ranch a man came out the front door with a shotgun. "Who are you mister and what do you want?"

John said, "Is this the Sanger ranch?"

The man said "Yes it's the Sanger-Stanton ranch now."

Just then another man came out, "What's going on here?"

He spied John and said, "Orin is that you? Son, have you finally come home?"

Cal Rankin came running up to Ole Satan and practically pulled Orin off his saddle. They hugged each other and laughed and cried.

Finally John pulled loose and said, "What did that man mean when he said the Sanger-Stanton ranch?"

Cal said, "Come inside Orin we have a lot of talking to do."

"Where's Pa, Cal?"

Cal said, "He's lying along side of your Ma out back son. Come on I'll explain."

They went inside and talked long into the night. About two years after Orin had left the territory, Major Stanton had a change of heart. He told the law the truth about what had happened. He even got a full pardon from the territorial governor for the three men Orin had killed who were torturing the young Indian boy.

"Your father and Major Stanton became good friends. They sent riders out to give you the news but no one had ever heard of Orin Sanger wherever they went. Now I know why you became John Stanton and had a whole new life ahead of you. I'm sorry about your wife and baby in Montana, John. I'm going to call you John now if you don't mind."

John nodded yes.

"Major Stanton suggested that they join together and run cattle. Your father thought it would be a good idea. They became partners. That includes you. The Major fired his foreman because he suspected he had something to do with the cattle rustling going on in the territory. Someone was hitting all of the ranches. They would only take the strays that they found. They left the main herds alone. That's why they weren't detected right away."

Cal went on, "Six weeks ago the Major was having a pipe of tobacco on his front porch after dinner and someone shot him in the back as he was entering the house. The shooter wasn't found. The Major was helping his niece with her college tuition and she left school to take care of him. The ex-foreman came out to the ranch to offer a buyout to the Major. He refused naturally and the ex-foreman tried to get the girl to convince the Major to sell. She told him to get out and leave them alone. He left fuming."

John asked, "How is the Major doing, Cal?"

Not so good. The doctors here are afraid to operate because he could become paralyzed and he won't go east and leave the ranch unguarded."

John said, "I'm going to see the Major now."

Cal replied, "I'm going with you. The ranch hands don't know you and they might shoot first and ask questions later."

They arrived at the Major's ranch and with Cal explaining who he was they were allowed onto the property without incident. The Major and his niece Carrie were sitting on the front porch reading. The Major had lost a lot of weight and had aged considerably. Carrie Stanton on the other hand was a very pretty and well groomed young lady.

Cal made the introductions.

The Major spoke first. He apologized for everything that had happened to make Orin leave the territory. He explained how he and Walt Sanger had become friends and then partners.

"We combined both ranches and have been very successful. Your name is on the deed along with Carrie, my niece, and I. You are going to become a very rich young man."

He went on, "If you aren't satisfied we can put your name on the Sanger ranch in your name only. It's up to you. I'm just following your father's wishes in this matter."

John was overwhelmed. He didn't know what to say. The Major went on, "Cal told me about your name change and some of your exploits and from the long talks I had with your father, you are exactly like him."

John said, "What do you mean."

The Major replied, "In his younger days your father was a very famous lawman. He was in many gunfights and walked away from all of them in one piece. The killings were playing on his mind and one day he was confronted by a young man who wanted to make a name for himself. He challenged your father. Your father tried to reason with him but to no avail. The young man drew on him but your father drew and killed him first. After that your father decided he couldn't do it anymore. He knew that there would be more young men willing to do the same. He hung up his guns and left the territory. He ended up going to Montana for a while but he got homesick for Texas and started home. He came across a wagon train, with a load of Quakers looking for a place to settle. He hired on as a hunter and guide. That's where he met your mother. They fell in love. They wanted to get married. Your mother's parents were agreeable but wanted to know more about your father and his past."

"Your father explained about his former life and asked a big favor of your grandfather. When he married he wanted to take the bride's surname as his own. Your grandfather agreed and he became Walt Sanger. Your mother was happy that she didn't have to change her name.

John asked, "I wonder why my father never told me about that part of his life?"

The Major said, "He didn't want to influence you to be like him and wear a gun."

Cal spoke up, "That's right John, your father was the fastest gun I'd ever seen until you showed me different."

"When you came out of that barn loaded for bear your father was both proud and scared for you. He was also angry at me for teaching you how to shoot. I don't know how he figured it out; he took that to the grave."

The Major said, "Orin, or John, whichever you prefer, you are now running the largest ranch in this part of the territory. I'm making Cal foreman of the combined ranches. How does that suit you?"

"Well, Major, it's an offer I'm going to accept on one condition. You go back east with your niece to one of the best doctors available or better yet we'll have him come here to operate. We have to get you well. This ranch is too big for one man to run."

They agreed on everything. The doctor was sent for and would arrive in a few weeks. The deed was changed so that all three people who were listed on it were Stanton's.

John went to Abilene to open a new account at the bank. After making all of the arrangements he went to the local saloon with Cal to enjoy a beer. When they were leaving a large man came in the door and bumped into John. The man almost fell because John stood his ground.

The man was belligerent. He screamed out, "Watch where you are going you ignorant clod. Do you know who I am?"

John said, No and I don't think I want to know either."

Cal spoke up, "John this is Mel Stuart, he used to be foreman at the Major's ranch."

Stuart said, "I've got my own ranch now, Rankin, and this clod owes me an apology."

John turned to leave but Stuart grabbed him by the arm and said "Apologize now or in the street. It's up to you."

John said, "I'll meet you outside."

He and Cal left the saloon. Stuart took off his coat and checked his holster. When he turned to go outside one of his men took his arm and said, "Mr. Stuart do you know who that man is?"

He said, "No, why should that bother me?"

The man answered, "When I knew him a few years back his name was John Stanton. He's the fastest gun I've ever seen."

Stuarts face was ashen. "You mean the lawman gunfighter John Stanton?"

"Yessir, the one and only. I saw him do in three men at the same time. It's him alright."

Stuart took off his gun and holster and went outside. He showed John that he wasn't armed and said, "I was hasty in there sir and I apologize for what I did and said."

John accepted his apology and left to enjoy the sights of Abilene. It had been quite a while since he'd seen the place. He gave the recorded deed and all of the bank papers to Cal and sent him to the ranch.

He said, "I'm going to spend a few days looking up old friends."

Cal left for the ranch. Meanwhile Mel Stuart looked up the man who had given him information about John Stanton.

"What's your name boy?"

The man answered, "Duke, sir, Duke Crane."

"Well Duke Crane, you work for me, right?"

"Yessir."

"You do as you're told and you'll be rich beyond anything you ever dreamed about and I'll have the reputation I've always wanted to have and need at this time."

Duke smiled and said, "Whatever you want boss, I'm your man."

Mel asked, "Well first off, where is there a quiet place where men can settle their differences without any problems?"

Duke informed, "I think the stables west of town would be best. People don't like to go near there because of the smell and all."

Mel went on, "Good, I want you to find a good place to hide and when you hear John Stanton and I coming, be ready. You are going to hear me count to three. When I reach two, I want you to shoot John Stanton and then leave as quickly as you can. I want to be alone to explain what happened here. Got it?"

Duke nodded and left to find a good place to hide.

Mel Stuart found John Stanton at the hardware store. He confronted him outside, "I've been thinking about how you pushed me and I still feel that you owe me an apology."

"No way am I going to apologize for your rotten behavior."

"Well I guess I know where that leaves us, but we shouldn't settle the matter here. Some innocent person could be hurt. Let's go behind the stables over there and settle this quickly."

A few moments later they went behind the stables and Mel Stuart took off his coat and repeated, "It's not too late to apologize, cowboy. Do it now or I count to three and we'll have at it."

John said, "Start counting."

Stuart started counting. Both men were tense. "One…Two…"

As soon as he reached two a shot rang out from the roof of the stable and John Stanton's hat flew off and blood started flowing.

Stuart drew his gun and fired as soon as he could but he was firing at his man on the roof. He heard him cry out. He was going to check him out but he heard people coming to the stables. He stopped and turned to greet them.

He said, "Sorry folks but this rowdy wouldn't accept my apology for bumping into him. He challenged me and got what he deserved."

When they saw all the blood around John's head they turned and walked away.

Stuart saw an Indian standing near the stable. He pointed at him and said, "You, Indian, take this body and bury it in the cemetery at the edge of town. I'll give you a few dollars when you bring his horse back."

The Indian did as he was told. He loaded the bloody body on the horse and led him off out of town. He recognized Orin Sanger immediately and saw that he was still alive. Head wounds always bleed profusely. Everyone assumed that he was dead.

He quickly dug a shallow grave and put rocks in it. He shoveled dirt back over it and piled more rocks on it and drove a stick in the ground to mark it. He hung Orin's hat from it. He then rode off out of town and rode to their mountain hideout.

When John woke up two days later the wound had been tended to and he was well on the way to recovery.

White Fox greeted him, "Hello my cousin Sanger. How is it with you?"

John smiled and said, "It is good to see you my cousin White Fox."

He then explained to his cousin how he had been shot before the man reached the number three. He was shot from behind.

White Fox muttered, "White man's treachery again."

"Would you like me to avenge you cousin, I have become quite fast with my gun."

"No," John answered, "I want to see the look on his face when he sees me again."

One week later a stronger, and much more resolute, John Stanton, was ready. White Fox saddled a horse and offered to go with him, but John said no. He didn't want to involve the tribe with his problems. They had enough of their own.

John arrived at the Stanton's ranch. Everyone thought that he was dead and buried. They even had a service and erected a cross over his gravesite.

John was making his plans when one of the ranch hands came to the house and told him that Mel Stuart and his men were going to be there in the morning. He would have the sheriff and a judge with him this time. He had signed papers declaring him as the owner of the Sanger ranch.

The papers were a bill of sale from the son with his signature on them. He would own the water rights and eventually block out the Stanton ranch from using the water. He would then offer to buy the Stanton ranch at a considerable savings to himself.

"Where did you learn this?" John asked.

"One of Stuart's men told me. He's the one who shot you on orders from Mel Stuart. Stuart is trying to find him to keep him quiet. He tried to shoot him the day he had him shoot you, but it didn't work out. He kept in touch with one of Stuart's hands and he told him what Stuart is planning to do. He quit Stuart's bunch too."

"Where are they now?" John asked

"They are about one hundred yards east in that stand of trees."

John said, "Go get them I don't want anything happening to either one of them."

Duke Crane came in with hands in the air. John said, "Put your hands down. You don't have anything to fear from me. Have you figured out why Stuart tried to kill you?"

"Yessir, Mr. Stanton he wanted everyone to think he outdrew you and shot you himself. I was the only other one who knew what had happened."

Duke went on, "I would have done anything for that man. He's the first one to give me a good paying job. I'm a little slow and he didn't make fun of me for it. I'm not a good shot but I can ride herd on cows.

John said, "Well I'm thanking the good Lord for your poor shooting and I forgive you in front of all of these witnesses. I'm going to ask you to testify to all of this in front of a judge. I'll see that you don't get any jail time."

"Yessir," Duke said.

"If you need a cow punching job that doesn't include shooting we can use you both here. Get out to the bunkhouse and find a place for yourselves. I'll need you here when Stuart comes in the morning."

They left for the bunkhouse.

Cal said, "How do you want to play this out John?"

John said, "Take the Major and Carrie out to one of the line shacks."

They immediately protested but he told them he couldn't guarantee their safety if there was any shooting. They reluctantly agreed.

John turned to Cal, "Place some good riflemen in a few strategic spots. I want everyone covered who comes in to the ranch. They don't know that I'm still alive so you answer the door."

Cal smiled and nodded. He could hardly wait.

They came just before noon the next day. Stuart pounded on the door. Cal opened it and Stuart, the sheriff, and judge walked in.

Stuart smiled at Cal and said, "I have an order for you and your men to vacate the old Sanger ranch and I'm sure the Major will have you leave here also."

Cal said, "Why should I believe you? The Sanger ranch is family owned. The Major is also a partner in it."

"Not anymore Cal, I bought the ranch from the young Sanger and I have the deed to prove it." He turned to the sheriff and said "Serve the papers sheriff."

John's voice boomed out of the back room, "You are all covered. Reach for your guns and we will shoot!"

Everyone froze.

John came into the room and approached the sheriff, "Well guess who we have here, Cal? This is the sheriff form Montana that I was telling you about. He's wanted by the Federal Marshall's for murder, bank robbery, and rustling."

He leaned forward and took the sheriff's gun. John turned to the judge and said, "Your Honor I don't know if you are in with this bunch or not. I hope for your sake you aren't."

"No Sir", the judge said, "These men made me come with them because of the legal problems that might arise. Who might you be, young man?"

"Well your Honor, since my father Walt Sanger died and I'm his only heir. I'm the only one who can sign off on that deed and I guarantee that I didn't."

Mel Stuart was backing out the door when he felt a six gun at his back. He turned to find all of his men with their hands in the air and their weapons at their feet.

The man with the gun was Duke Crane.

"Quick," Stuart said, "give me your gun."

Duke laughed and said, "I don't think Mr. Stanton would like that. I work for him now."

Everyone came out to the porch. The judge was telling John Stanton that he was free of all legal obligations as far as Mel Stuart was concerned.

John called out to Stuart, "We have something to settle Stuart. Let's get on with it."

Stuart hollered out at the judge, "You can't leave me here. I can't draw on him, it would be murder."

The judge said, "You made your bed, you can just lie in it." The judge rode off.

Stuart opened his coat, "I don't have a gun so you can't draw on me."

John turned to say something to Cal. Stuart reached under his coat behind his back and drew a gun that had been in his belt. Two shots rang out and Stuart hit the ground face first.

John and Cal reached for their guns but Dukes voice spoke up, "Wow, that's the best shooting I ever did Mr. Stanton." The smoke was still curling up from his gun barrel.

John laughed and said, "That's the second time your shooting saved my life.

A MONTH LATER...

The Major was recovering nicely from the operation. The ranch was doing well and everything was fine. John received a letter forwarded from the bank in Abilene from Carl Johnson, Maggie's husband.

Maggie has died of a broken heart. When Lizzie and her baby died, she started to die herself along with them. I'm selling the ranch. I'm forwarding your share to the bank in Abilene.

I had Maggie buried in the church cemetery. I had Lizzie moved there alongside of her. It was her last request. I hope this sets well with you. I hope all is well with you and your family. It was a pleasure to know you.

~ Carl Johnson

A bank messenger came to the ranch and notified John that a considerable deposit was made to his account. Four months later Major Stanton gave his niece to John Stanton in marriage.

The Major thought to himself, "I never expected the Stanton name would be carried on like this. Who could have known?"   ... *THE END*

Made in the USA
Middletown, DE
28 January 2017